The Cellar Lad

ABBEY DALE WORKS, near SHEFFIELD.

DEALER in all kinds of CUTLERY, &c.

CONVERTER and REFINER of STEEL.

BOUGHT of JOHN DYSON,
LATE VICKERS, CARR, & DYSON.

Manufacturer of Scythes, Hay & Straw Knives, Knives for Straw Machines, Saws, Files, Edge Tools, and Garden Tools.

Theresa Tomlinson

The Cellar Lad

Julia MacRae Books

LONDON SYDNEY AUCKLAND JOHANNESBURG

First published 1995

1 3 5 7 9 10 8 6 4 2

Copyright © 1995 Theresa Tomlinson

Theresa Tomlinson has asserted her right
under the Copyright, Designs and Patents Act, 1988
to be identified as the author of this work

First published in Great Britain 1995
by Julia MacRae
an imprint of Random House
20 Vauxhall Bridge Road, London SW1V 2SA

Random House Australia (Pty) Ltd
20 Alfred Street, Milsons Point, Sydney, NSW 2061, Australia

Random House New Zealand Ltd
18 Poland Road, Glenfield, Auckland, New Zealand

Random House South Africa (Pty) Ltd
PO Box 337, Bergvlei 2012, South Africa

Random House UK Limited Reg. No 954009

A cip catalogue record for this book is
available from the British Library

ISBN 1 85681 581 1

Typeset by SX Composing Ltd, Rayleigh, Essex
Printed in England by Clays Ltd, St Ives plc

Contents

Also by Theresa Tomlinson

How like a stithy is this land!
And we lie on it like good metal
Long hammer'd by a senseless hand!

Ebenezer Elliott, from Goethe, 1834

Introduction

IN THE YEAR 1842 Sheffield was the main centre for the cutlery and tools industry. There were many political groups active in the rapidly expanding city. Chartists, Trade Unions, and the Anti-Corn Law League were all seeking to improve the lot of working families. Some people would have belonged to all three groups, while others might support just one cause. These groups worked independently, but would unite at times over a shared concern.

In 1838 the London Working Men's Association drew up a People's Charter, comprising of six points and demanding:
1. Universal male suffrage.
2. The secret ballot.
3. Equal electoral districts.
4. Abolition of the property qualification for MPs.
5. Payment of MPs.
6. Annual general elections.

Although these ideas had been raised before, they had never been put together in an organised way. The Chartists quickly gained support from working people throughout the country. In 1839 they presented their Charter to Parliament with 1.2 million signatures. It was rejected, as were two later petitions in 1842, and 1848.

Although at the time it looked as though Chartism had failed, we now have the first five points of the People's Charter at the heart of our system of democracy, along with votes for women. The sixth point of the Charter would be hard to put into practice!

There were by then Trade Unions in existence and members paid Union dues. In return the Unions would work to keep wages steady, improve working conditions, pay out sickness benefits, and maintain a high quality of goods produced. Employers who took on non-Union labour in order to pay them at a cheaper rate were bitterly resented by the Unions particularly during a period of depression. In order to enforce Union rules, artisans felt themselves morally justified in using non-violent pressure, ie. warning letters, removal of grinding belts, locally known as 'rattening'. These rattenings were not officially sanctioned by the Unions, so that individuals would be held responsible if caught. The heads of the Unions denounced the use of gunpowder or violence, but did not discourage the milder forms of rattening.

The Corn Law or Bread Tax prohibited the import of corn until home grown corn had reached 80 shillings a quarter. These laws were bitterly resented by the working classes because they kept the price of bread high even when wages dropped, bringing real hunger to poor families. An Anti-Corn Law League was founded.

This is a very brief and simple explanation of a complex and fascinating subject.

FOR MY FATHER - ALAN JOHNSTON

CHAPTER ONE

The Charcoal Burner's Grave

His books were rivers, woods and skies,
The meadow and the moor;

Ebenezer Elliott

SHARP SUNLIGHT cut down through the trees, but Ben still
shivered. It was chilly, even for April, though fat clumps
of primroses patterned the grass and delicate white wood
anemones raised purple stained caps. Ben hurried through
Ecclesall Woods, clutching his new linen work jacket about
him. The sun was high in the sky but still he hurried. He was
determined to find the charcoal burners. They should be
setting up camp deep in the woods for they usually arrived at
the beginning of April. Ben had been looking for them for
weeks now, and this was his last chance to find them; his last
day of freedom.

Tomorrow he was to start work; he'd be taking Jake
Thornton's place as cellar lad in the crucible workshop.
Tomorrow he'd be running around at everyone's beck and call.
So today was special; he must explain to Green Mort and his
family.

Ben swore under his breath as he tripped over dry brown
trailing brambles. They scratched his bare ankle with needle-
sharp thorns, making him stumble clumsily into marshy
ground.

Now his new clogs were coated with thick brown mud and his good fustian working breeches spattered. His nan would be sure to turn red in the face and yell at him.

Water, that was what he needed.

The marshy patches always appeared where trickles of water overflowed from the streams. He strode towards the faint gurgling sound and soon splashed down into a wide pool. He gritted his teeth as the water stung. But Ben was tough, he'd suffered worse than scratched ankles in his eleven years of life. He stood there in the water gently slopping his clogs up and down, sighing with relief as the pain faded and his shoes washed clean. He lifted his head and suddenly smiled with satisfaction. A wisp of smoke came curling through the fresh green leaves of a clump of alders.

"Charcoal burners," he whispered. "I knew it."

He splashed out of the water and set off in the direction of the smoke, slowly working his way deeper and deeper into the woods.

"What's up wi'them," he muttered. They didn't usually set up camp so far from the wide carters' road.

His eyes began to water as thin twirls of smoke grew into thick choking white clouds that puthered through the trees.

Can't have been here long, he thought. That was clear enough. It was always like this when they first set the stacks burning. The starting up was the worst bit; the smokiest bit. In a few days time all those smothering clouds would have cleared, leaving a fine blue haze hovering over the slow burning wood.

At last he stood at the edge of a clearing where five bell-shaped wood stacks smoked steadily beneath their covering of green turves. Ben clamped his hands tightly over his face to stop himself from coughing. No wonder folk called them the

Devil's Chimneys. The burning made no sound and though there was one small cone-shaped hut, Ben could see no sign of Mort or his family.

It was quiet, too quiet.

Green Mort brought his wife and their six children to camp in the woods throughout the summer months. The woodland around the chosen clearing usually rang with shouts and laughter as the charcoal burner's children played catch and built dens and climbed trees.

Back in Dyson's Scythe Works where Ben lived, he was surrounded by noise and plenty of it. There was the whirr of grinding wheels, the clang of scythe forging, and the deafening bursts of thunder that came from the tilt hammers; not to mention the raucous shouts of laughter of Jess and the packing women. The deep silence of the charcoal burner's clearing was quite strange and frightening.

All at once Ben's heart thumped for he saw that the stacks were watched after all; and he was not alone. A thin man with a soot-blackened face was sitting there, leaning against the hut. He kept himself as still as stone. He was hard to see for his clothes were faded green, the same dull shades as the dried out turves that covered his hut.

Ben spied on him from the shelter of a low holly bush.

"Where's Green Mort?" he whispered.

The man was not really watching the stacks as he should have been, his attention was taken by something else. Ben crept forward dodging from bush to bush, curiosity getting the better of fear. The man was reading a book. That was more surprising than anything. A charcoal burner reading a book!

Ben watched for a long time, his legs beginning to ache with the effort of keeping still; the sharp holly spikes pricking him whenever he made the slightest movement. He looked up and squinted through the bobbing green tips of the branches. The sun had travelled well across the sky towards the west. His day of freedom would soon be over.

All at once his attention was caught by the sounds of harsh coughing. The loose wooden hurdle that formed the door of the charcoal burner's hut flopped forward and rested on the stick that had been set there to catch it. The familiar sound of Green Mort's voice came to him across the clearing.

"Could sleep all day," Mort grumbled. "But I dare say you'd be complaining."

He came yawning and stretching from the hut.

"Light'll be going soon," the thin man said, shutting his book with a thump.

Ben strode towards them, gaining courage from the appearance of his friend. He cleared his throat politely, making both men look over at him.

"Ben!" Green Mort smiled broadly and went to clap him on the shoulder. "Grand to see thee, lad."

The new charcoal burner got to his feet. He was very tall as well as thin. His face was dirty, but his eyes were clear blue and he watched Ben steadily all the while.

"Wondered how long you were going to stay there behind that holly," he said.

Ben felt foolish. "I was looking for John and Ned."

Green Mort sighed. "The Missus won't come this year; she's expecting another bairn. Our John's gone to work over Wharncliffe way, and Ned's been taken on as a cooper's apprentice. So here I am with Lanky Dan. He comes from Nottingham way and he usually works near Sherwood."

"Sherwood!" Ben stared at the man with new interest.

Mort laughed. "Nay lad! He may wear green, but he's not Robin Hood. They call him the Book-Fuddler."

"Book-Fuddler!" Ben was puzzled.

Both the charcoal burners laughed.

"You know what a Fuddler is?" Mort asked.

"Aye," said Ben doubtfully. He'd heard his nan speak of drunken men being fuddled with drink.

"Fuddlers spend their earnings getting blind drunk," said Mort. "This feller spends his money in the second-hand bookshops."

Ben was amazed.

"That's right," said Lanky Dan. "Books. That's what keeps me going! I get wild and cheerful reading 'em. Sometimes I get angry, too."

"Well!" said Ben. He was speechless at the thought of such a thing. Whatever would his nan think of that? She certainly thought drunken fuddlers the lowest of the low.

"It's my missus' idea," said Green Mort. "She made me promise that I'd not work alone. Not after what happened to poor old George."

Ben nodded. He understood that all right. Everyone knew the dreadful story of George, who'd left his charcoal stacks and gone to drink at the Rising Sun alehouse. Somehow next morning his hut had been burned down and poor George with it. Some said that he'd been so drunk that he'd fallen into his fire, others that he'd been too drunk to beat out sparks that had blown on to his hut. Nobody knew the real truth of it. His drinking companions had been so upset that they'd raised a good sum of money and had a carved gravestone put out there in the woods. They were determined that George should not be forgotten.

Ben had often stared at the carefully made inscription, wondering what the words meant and wishing that he could read them. Suddenly Ben realised that maybe his chance had come.

He looked shyly up at the Book-Fuddler. "You can read," he said. "You could read George's grave?"

The man raised his sooty eyebrows in surprise. "I suppose I could! Where is this grave, then?"

The grey carved stone stood amongst young saplings. Ben felt a little uncomfortable alone with the Book-Fuddler. Mort had

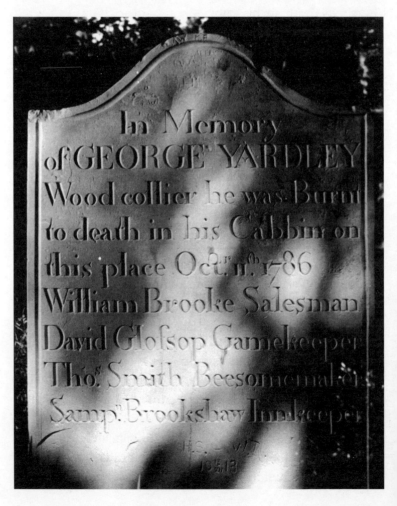

stayed behind to watch the stacks.

The tall man stood before the lonely grave set so deep in the woods, his thin face solemn. He pulled his cap from his head and cleared his throat. Then he spoke out in deep and ringing tones as though he addressed a great crowd, making Ben jump.

"'In Memory of George Yardley, wood collier. He was burnt to death in his cabin on this place, Oct 11th 1786. William Brooke, salesman, David Glossop, gamekeeper, Thos Smith, beesome maker, Samson Brookshaw, innkeeper.' Well . . . that's what it says, lad. They must have thought a lot of him. Would cost a pretty penny, this would."

Ben blinked hard. For some reason he suddenly wanted to cry. They stood side by side in silence for a while, the light fading fast; Ben's day of freedom gone. At last he stirred himself, remembering why he'd come into the woods in the first place.

"I meant to tell Mort that I have to start work tomorrow."

"Aye," said the man, unsurprised. "I thought as much. New clogs on your feet; new work jacket."

"I used to come running through the woods with Ruth," said Ben. "We came to play with Mort's little uns."

The man sighed. "No more running through the woods," he said.

"No," said Ben. "I'd better go."

He left the man still standing there in front of George's grave and strode off in the direction that he thought he'd come from. The silence and the gathering darkness seemed to thicken around him. At last he started to run but that set strange frightening woodland sounds trailing after him. Which way! Which way! Surely he couldn't be lost! His heart began to thump. He couldn't catch his breath. Then he heard it; a sound that warmed him right through to his very stomach. The regular thud of the plating hammer starting up after its seven minutes rest. It banged away in the distance as Ben slowed down, smiling at his own foolishness. He turned to walk confidently in the direction of the Scythe Works. He was not lost. How could he ever be lost, when he lived in such a place. A place that filled the whole valley with the thunderous sounds of its work.

CHAPTER TWO

The Cellar Lad

N AN WAS in a right old taking when Ben got back. She was banging pots about and spilling water on the freshly scrubbed kitchen floor. Ben hesitated by the back door of the small workman's cottage.

"I'm sorry," he panted. "I forgot the time. I never meant to be late."

Nan looked up at him, puzzled, as though he were the last person she'd expected to see.

"Ben? Oh aye . . . I see it's dark! You're late, lad."

Ben sighed with relief. Nan was forgetful at times. It was clearly not his lateness that had put her into a fretful mood. He should have kept his mouth shut and she'd not have noticed.

"I'll get the bowls and spoons, Nan," he hastened to soothe her.

"Aye, and will you fetch a jug of ale from Widow Blackitt's? Your father'll be here any minute and I want his dinner to be ready for him and a good drink of ale to go with it."

Ben snatched up the empty jug and set off for the small alehouse, past the Works' gates, where Mrs Blackitt kept an open door to all the Scythe workers' families.

"Now then, Ben," said Widow Blackitt as she filled his jug. "From what I hear you'll be doing plenty o' fetching ale before long." She was a fat cheerful woman who talked non-stop.

Ben nodded and sighed. "That's right. I've to start in the morning," he said.

Ben knew that the cellar lad must spend half his time fetching great buckets of barley ale. As far as the melting team were concerned, that was a cellar lad's most important job. The men worked so hard and in such great heat that the sweat poured out of their skin. It was only large supplies of good barley ale that could keep them from fainting. Plain water would have made them sick and brought their skin out in blisters; white canker, as they called it.

"Now remember," said Widow Blackitt. "This may not be the biggest alehouse hereabouts, but it's the nearest and my ale is the best. Will I be seeing you in the morning, then?"

"Aye," said Ben.

"That's my lad," she pinched his cheek.

When Ben got home, he found his father sitting at the table, all washed and ready to eat. His father was the pot man at the Scythe Works. He made the great vase-like pots that the crucible men melted their steel in. Each night he came home exhausted and covered with clay dust. He had to strip off his clothes and wash himself down at the big stone sink while Nan brought him hot water from the fire.

Ben sniffed and smiled. A grand smell of cooking filled the cottage. Nan was ladling sheep's head stew and dumplings into three bowls.

"Come on, lad," she said. "Get sat down before it goes cold."

She stood watching them both with her hands on her hips, waiting until they'd eaten a few spoonfuls, then she sat down and spoke determinedly.

"Now look here, Frank, it's really worrying me sick is this petition they're all on about. I don't want you going and putting your mark on it. It could be dangerous. We've never been ones for book learning in our family. You can't write your name, no more than I can."

"Well, Mother, that's where you're wrong," Frank Sterndale waved his spoon at her. "I *can* write my name, and so can all the melting team, now. Jess's been helping us. We've learnt to make our marks, drawing out the letters in my clay pit. Now what do you think of that?"

Ben stared from one to the other. He knew well enough what his father was talking about. All of Sheffield could talk of little else. A great petition was to be taken down to London by the Chartists and carried through the streets to Parliament. They wanted all men to be given the right to vote, and this weekend was the last chance there'd be for those wishing to put their names to it. Ben was surprised to hear his father disagree with Nan. Though Frank was well respected at the Scythe Works, Nan was the boss at home, no doubt of that.

"Oh dear," Nan sighed. "If Mr Dyson finds out there'll be trouble I swear."

"Stop fretting, Mother," Frank shook his head. "Dyson would be hard put to find himself another pot man. He'd be hard put to find himself another melting team to make his steel."

"Aye, maybe," Nan shook her head. "But what about the grinders? He can find himself more grinders just like that!" She snapped her fingers.

Frank Sterndale nodded, his face serious. "You're right about that; the grinders are risking most, but they're more determined than any of us. Stop fretting. Dyson shan't know which of his workers signed or not. You won't find his name on the list!"

"Now if it were the bread tax that you were objecting to, I'd be thinking you were quite right!" Nan was well known for her anger at the way the price of bread was kept high, even when wages fell.

"Eh, Mother!" Frank sighed. "Can't you see? If only working men could vote and sit in Parliament, they'd get rid of that wicked bread tax straight away. They'd get rid of the Workhouse, too. That's why we need our Charter so."

Nan huffed and fussed, her face pink with the worry of it. "It won't do any good! Look what happened last time? Parliament turned the petition away without even looking at it!"

"They didn't understand it," said Frank. "They didn't know how folks were suffering! This time they'll listen . . . this time they must!"

The next morning Ben's father woke him just as dawn was breaking. Though he didn't much fancy the thought of leaving his warm bed, he stumbled obediently down the ladder from the loft where he slept and went out to wash at the pump. He worked the handle up and down until bursts of icy water shot all over his face and neck.

"Ah . . . ah," he yelled, shaking his head so that water flicked all over the yard.

"Don't you waste good water," his father called.

Nan had got up to make them both a bowl of porridge and by the time Ben was dressed and ready in his new clogs, he began to feel excited. This was a big day for him. He was a worker at last and taking on a proper job. There was only one cellar lad in the Scythe Works and that was him, Ben Sterndale. Jake Thornton, the last cellar lad, had been promoted to the melting team.

"You do as you're told," said his father as they walked across the cobbled yard to the crucible workshop. "You do as you're told and impress the melter, then you'll maybe get a chance to join the melting team like Jake. Or I might even take you on as second pot man if you shape up well with the clay. Whatever you do, you take notice of old Joe, the puller-out."

"Oh," said Ben. "I thought the melter was Head of Shop."

"Aye. So he is, but Joe knows more about making crucible steel than anyone else I know. You'll see, even the melter takes notice of what he says. He used to work with the Huntsman family when he were a lad."

Ben was impressed. "What? Benjamin Huntsman that worked out how to make our steel in pots?"

"Aye," his father's voice was low with reverence. "Benjamin Huntsman, who we named you for."

"Right," said Ben. "I will take notice of the puller-out."

Ben started the day working in the pot shop with his father, helping him carefully to mix up the powdered clay and water in the pit on the floor. His father pulled off his boots, then, after rolling up his trouser legs, he stepped into the clay pit. Ben shuddered at the sight of the wet clay slipping and squelching beneath his father's bare feet.

"No need for that sour face." Frank laughed as he started the rhythmic treading of the clay. "It's the only way to get it right."

As soon as the cokey arrived to stoke up the fires, Ben was sent to help the melting team. The day turned into a wild blur as he was sent running down into the cellar to rake out the hearths, then called up into the melting shop. Down he went into the cellars again for more hearth raking, then out to Widow Blackitt's for ale. He had to pass Jess and the gang of women who worked in the yard, packing the newly oiled and

MAKING CRUCIBLES FOR MELTING.   TREADING THE CLAY.

blackened scythes into wooden crates filled with straw.

"'Ello, Benny," they teased. "Fetch some ale for us, will yer? Elsie's got a terrible thirst on 'er . . . 'aven't you, Elsie?"

Then when he got back they smacked their lips and threatened to steal a sup of ale from the two heavy buckets that he carried slung from his shoulders on a wooden yoke.

"Give us some ale and we'll give you a kiss!"

"Take no notice of them," called Mr Price from the tilt forge where he worked.

"I shan't," said Ben.

He swerved and ignored them, though his knees shook as he climbed the stone steps up into the workshop. As soon as the men had supped, he was sent down into the pot shop again to help his father with the clay. He must learn how to make the flat round lids for the crucibles, yet another part of a cellar lad's job, though the great pots must be left to his father.

"Phew!" he said. "Does a cellar lad have to do everything round here?"

His father laughed. "Aye, you're getting the idea. I think they're shouting for ale again."

Ben was still working on the clay lids at dusk though his head nodded and jerked. His father paused in his work and smiled at him. He put his big clay-dusted hand under the boy's chin.

"Go on, our Ben. Get yourself home before you drop into my pot and flatten it. You've done all right for a first day. Get yourself home."

"Now, Benny," the women shouted as he stumbled through the pecking hens and geese that scratched for corn in Dyson's Yard, "Who's a big workman now, Benny? Big enough for a sweetheart, ey? There's Elsie here needs a nice young man . . . don't you, Elsie?"

Elsie was a big woman, past fifty. "Aye," she shrieked. "I like 'em young and tender."

The packers screamed with laughter.

"Leave 'im be," Jess told them.

Ben grinned. He'd known them all his life. He wasn't going to let that lot scare him now.

He stopped as he reached the cottage door and stared up at the wooded hillsides that surrounded the Scythe Works. No more running wild through the woods. He wasn't unhappy. Though every muscle in his body ached, he'd got through his first day and managed not to disgrace himself.

Nan was fast asleep in the rocking chair. Her mouth had fallen open and she snored gently. Ben stood quietly beside her. Nan's blue checked working gown was worn with constant rubbing and scrubbing, but it was spotless, as was the snowy white apron fastened round her waist. A thin wisp of white hair crept from her close-fitting linen cap.

She was a strict old lady and she often got cross and exasperated with him, but she'd cooked and cleaned and kept their small cottage spick and span ever since Ben's mother had died of the terrible cholera sickness soon after he'd been born. Nan was the closest thing to a mother that Ben had got. He noticed sadly how thin her hands had grown, with blue veins standing out clearly amongst the brown patches that came with age.

Ben crept out to the pump to wash away the day's grime.

CHAPTER THREE

The Petition

Avenge the plunder'd poor, oh Lord!
But not with fire, but not with sword.

Ebenezer Elliott

B Y THE END of the first week, Ben was beginning to get the hang of the job. The cellar lad was everybody's servant, he'd expected that; but he hadn't realised how dizzy he'd be with the orders that were bellowed at him.

It was worst when they all shouted at once.

"Where's that Nipper?"

"Get yersel' here . . . boy!"

"Where's that damn cellar lad?"

At first he hadn't known which way to turn, but he soon learned that the melter must be obeyed first; then the puller-out.

Widow Blackitt was a grand help, and even though his shoulders ached with the weight of the yoke and the full buckets, Ben looked forward to the call for ale. However rushed he was, the old lady made him sit down while she opened her barrel.

"Now," she said, smiling broadly and winking, "I always say the cellar lad must have a little sip, just to test it out. You've got to make sure it's best ale, haven't you?"

Ben nodded, eagerly taking the small mug that she offered to him.

"They'll all be yelling at me," he told her. "They'll be
shouting, 'Where's the ale? Have you been brewing it?' "

"Take no notice," said Widow Blackitt. "Just tell 'em that
you have to walk slow, for they don't want their precious ale
spilled over your clogs, do they? Tell 'em Widow Blackitt says
so."

"Aye. I'll tell 'em," said Ben, as he shouldered the wooden
yoke.

And when they complained, he did tell them boldly what the
alewife had said. They cursed and slapped him on the back
with cheerful good humour.

By Saturday night Ben was worn out. He'd never longed for
the peace of Sunday before. Though he dare not tell his father
so, he was very clear about one thing; he hated Joe the puller-
out.

The man was older than anyone else who worked at
Dyson's; his thin hair was grizzled with dirt and singed from
the sparks that flew up from the white hot steel. He spat
constantly. All too often his spittle flew straight to Ben's clogs;
Ben was sure he aimed it there. The muscles and veins in the
puller-out's long arms stood out like cabled rope. But bent and
gnarled though he was, the other men stood back respectfully
when Joe took up his heavy long-handled tongs and went to
pull out the crucible pots full of molten steel. Everyone held
their breath as he hauled the glowing pots up from the round
sunken furnace holes that were set into the floor of the melting
shop.

The melter looked to the puller-out to judge when a pot was
ready for pulling. He would not give the order to pour until the
old man had nodded his head and said, "Aye . . . it's ready. It's
killed."

28

The puller-out had a foul temper, and if the ale or water was not there the moment he wanted it, the cellar lad was landed a sharp clout. Ben didn't mind the cheerful teasing and roughness of the other men, but he shuddered when he heard the puller-out calling, "Where's that damned cellar lad?"

The first Saturday after Ben had started work, his father got up from the dinner table and set about washing himself and putting on his Sunday suit.

"Aren't you going down to Widow Blackitt's?" Ben asked puzzled.

"No," Nan answered for him, crossly. "He's off into town, getting himself into trouble. Putting his name on that petition."

Ben watched as his father nervously smoothed down his thinning brown hair. He winked at Ben.

"You should come with me, son. If you're old enough to do a good day's work, then I say that you're old enough to put your mark upon the page and ask that all men should have the vote."

"How can you, Frank? He's nowt but a bairn," Nan turned on him angrily.

Ben looked from one to the other. The last thing he wished to do was go walking all the way to Sheffield. He'd been planning to run off into the woods to find the charcoal burners; the first time for a whole week that he'd been free. But his father had spoken to him as though he were a man and not a child. He'd asked him, not told him, and Ben felt that his father really wanted his company.

"I can't write my name," he said, nervous at the thought of even trying.

"They've plenty of fellows will help you make your mark."

"You don't want to be trailing all the way to Sheffield," said Nan, hands on hips, her face red and concerned.

Ben smiled fondly at her. He landed a smacking kiss on the tip of her nose. "I'm going with my father," he said.

It was a sunny afternoon in the second week of May. The yard was quieter than usual, for the grinders had gone off to work at the Thorpe brothers' wheel while the main shaft of Dyson's grinding wheel was mended. Mr Dyson had been annoyed for he swore that the Thorpe brothers charged too much. Mr Dyson complained in general that grinders charged too much for their work, but the Grinders' Union was the most powerful of all the Sheffield Trades.

The packing women were cheered by the warmth of the sun, though it turned their faces pink and sweaty. Ben carried ale through the yard.

"Do y'see who we've got working here?" Jess called out to him. "You're not the only youngster with a job."

Ben turned around, surprised, and recognised Jess's daughter, Ruth. Jess had often left her in Nan's care when she'd been little, and she and Ben had played happy wild games together.

They smiled shyly now. Ruth was taller than Ben and she suddenly seemed very grown up to him, working there in the yard with the other women.

"She's started this morning," said Jess. "We were wondering when you'd notice."

Ruth giggled.

"Too busy," said Ben. "They're on at me all the time."

"She's got trouble with her hands," said Jess. "But then, we all start out like that."

Ben looked closely and was shocked to see that Ruth's hands

were sore and bleeding from the sharp dry straw that the women plaited and packed the finished scythes in.

He forgot his shyness and touched the raw base of her thumb, gently. "That's bad."

Ruth turned her hand and flinched. "They've been telling me they were the same. Just lasts a week or two. Takes a while to get your hands hardened."

"Told you what to do, little lass," said Elsie.

"They've been on at me to rub goose grease on my hands," said Ruth. "I daren't tell you what Elsie said to rinse my hands in." She giggled again.

Jess winked and pinched her nose. Ben pulled a face. He could guess, knowing Elsie.

"Where's that blasted cellar lad?"

Ben jumped, almost spilling the ale. It was the puller-out. He'd better get back to the workshop quickly, but as he climbed the steps, there came the sound of a pony's hooves and excited shouting behind him.

Jack Carter drove his pony and cart into the yard and pulled it sharply to a halt.

"Have you heard the news?" he shouted. "Parliament's turned the Charter down."

"What," cried Jess. "Are you sure?"

"Aye. Sheffield's buzzing with it."

Ben climbed the stone steps to the crucible workshop. The puller-out waved him impatiently over.

"They've turned the Charter down," he said, hoping to explain his lateness. "Jack Carter's just been telling us."

The puller-out swore under his breath but he spoke unusually kind.

"Come on then, lad, we'll be needing that ale more than ever."

The men stood about drinking. There was a good deal of cursing, but their voices were low, their faces grim. Ben shuffled his feet uncomfortably. Gloom seemed to fill every corner of the Works, almost as though somebody had died.

"Best tell my dad," he muttered.

"Aye," the melter nodded.

Ben clomped slowly down the winding stone steps to the pot shop and gave his father the news.

Frank Sterndale was finishing a new batch of crucible pots, pressing the metal shaper down to pull in the tops; making the bonnets, as he called them. He heaved a great sigh.

"Nay! Surely not! After all that work! All that effort! Your nan will be saying, 'I told you so.'"

"Aye. She will," Ben agreed.

He set about his work with a heaviness of heart. Surely it was only right, only just, that working men should have a vote. Who would speak for them now? Who would speak for those poor folk who'd stood patiently in their rags, waiting to put their marks on the petition.

He'd been amazed that Saturday in April when he'd gone into Sheffield with his father and seen that great line of people, waiting in a queue. Ben had seen poverty, but he'd never seen folk like them. There were grinders sick with the lung disease and file cutters with hunched backs and yellow skins; but they at least had decent clothes and boots to their feet. The worst were the unemployed; and Sheffield was full of them now that trade had slumped and jobs were few. They queued up in Paradise Square, their clothes in tatters, their feet bare, faces thin and drawn. Desperate men and worn-out women with skinny babies in their arms; hordes of hungry children clutching at their skirts. They waited nervously, shuffling towards the rough trestle tables piled high with sheets of paper.

"Look," said Ben. "There's our Maggie. They've brought all the bairns. Fancy doing that!"

They went to join Ben's older sister, with her husband who was a fork grinder, and stood with them in the waiting line. Ben spotted the Book-Fuddler at the front. He seemed to be helping people to sign.

"I know him," Ben told his father. "He's working with Green Mort in Ecclesall Woods."

"Is he? He must be a Chartist then, for that's Mr Harney that's standing beside him. He's grand at making speeches is Mr Harney."

Ben and his father moved slowly forwards with the rest. Frank Sterndale wrote his name, his tongue moving over his lips with the effort of it and his hand shaking all the while. Ben made a cross and the Book-Fuddler put beautiful neat letters beside it.

"What does that say?" Ben asked.

"Benjamin Sterndale, his mark," the Book-Fuddler told him, carefully pointing out each word.

Ben stared down at the curls and loops and dashes.

"Wish I could write," he said.

The Book-Fuddler pressed a fold of printed paper into his hand. "It's reading that you want first," he said. "See if you can learn your letters from this pamphlet!"

Ben returned to the Scythe Works, clutching his paper, glad that his mark would be sent all the way to London along with the hopes of so many.

Now the petition had been thrown out of Parliament, even though three million names were written on it with such great striving, and even though it had been carried through the streets of London by a huge crowd. The workers were quiet that night as they walked across Dyson's Yard.

Ben's father shook his head. "It's set me thinking about that young Chartist chap, Samuel Holberry. Can you remember him, Ben? He's in jail now, put to the treadmill so I've heard. We thought he were a wild lad, wanting a rebellion. He was planning to take over the town hall."

"Yes," said Ben, frowning. "I do seem to remember. Our Maggie knows his wife, doesn't she? Didn't somebody give their plans away?"

His father nodded and sighed. "Just makes you wonder if he wasn't so mad after all. They've worked like beasts, these Chartist chaps, travelling from place to place, making their speeches, getting folk to make their marks, all peaceable-like. Then Parliament turns up its nose and won't even look at our petition or our Charter! I start to think maybe poor Samuel was right!"

The puller-out, coming up behind them heard his words. "Course he were right," he snarled.

CHAPTER FOUR

News from Sheffield

DISAPPOINTMENT hung over the Scythe Works. According to Jack Carter it was the same throughout Sheffield Town. During the weeks that followed, Ben swore that the puller-out grew more foul-tempered than ever, and Nan was not her usual self. One evening at the end of May, Ben and his father returned from their day's work to find her in a real taking; banging her pans and slamming down spoons on the table.

"Whatever is it?" Frank Sterndale asked.

"It's news from our Maggie," she said. "That chap who lives next door to them has died."

"Eh dear. I'm sorry to hear that. Was it the grinders' sickness?"

"Aye. He's been failing these last two years, though our Maggie's been doing all she can to help him."

"Well," said Frank. "It's a bad thing and no mistake, but at least the poor fellow's out of pain. It'll be a bit easier for our Maggie now. She's enough to do, what with her expecting again."

Nan turned around her face quivering with indignation. "That's where you're wrong," she said. "Have you forgotten that the fellow had a bairn? You'd think one of his sisters would see to the child, but they won't. They say they've got their hands full with their own. But not our Maggie! Oh no! She's only gone and taken him in."

Ben and his father both sighed. At last they could

35

understand Nan's agitation. Maggie was not strong and she'd got four small children of her own to look after as well as the one soon to be born.

"Well," Nan went on angrily. "I've sent a message back to her with Jack Carter. I've told her that I'm going to take that child up to the House."

"Oh, Nan!" said Ben. "Not the Workhouse."

"Now don't you go thinking I like it," Nan wagged her finger in his face. "I don't like it at all, but I won't have our Maggie killing herself for someone else's brat. He's nowt but a baby and he'll never know any different."

Ben's father shook his head. "Those places," he said. "I don't like the thought of it, baby or no."

As the warmer weather came, work went steadily on at Dyson's Scythe Works even though trade was slow. One afternoon in June, the melting shop had grown so desperately hot that the faces and bodies of the workers streamed with sweat.

The melter went to lift up one of the furnace covers, making them all shrink back, their faces gleaming white in the glow. He turned to the puller-out. "I think this steel's about right. Shall we have the pot out?"

"Aye," the puller-out agreed. "Where's the Nipper?" he bellowed. "We'll wet our rags."

The two men went to the open doorway and Ben trotted obediently after them. He picked up the besom that always stood in the water trough and began to brush them down with water, soaking the thick sacking rags that they wore tied round their legs and arms for protection.

"Watch it," the puller-out snarled as Ben dribbled water down his heavy boots. "I'm not off swimming, tha daft lad," he grumbled. "Ale now . . . and quick about it."

Ben poured a mug of ale. He waited nervously while the men drank. Then he took the jug and backed away. If the steel was ready to be poured, he must stand still, he must not move a muscle; he could not take the chance of spilling ale near a crucible full of molten steel.

"All ready?" The puller-out had picked up his straight tongs.

"Aye," said the melter.

CASTING INGOTS.   DRAWING THE CRUCIBLES.

Slow and steady, the puller-out clamped his tongs on the top of the pot and drew the crucible upwards from its furnace hole in the floor. It came out glowing golden white through a coating of grey ash. The muscles knotted in his arms as he set it carefully down in the teeming bay.

He stood back a little then as the melter came to clamp his heavy curved tongs around the crucible pot.

Ben held his breath. Grunting with effort, the melter braced the weight against his thigh. The puller-out bent to skim the slag from the top of the molten steel with the iron bar that he called his mop.

Smoothly and steadily the white liquid steel was teemed into the mould. The workshop was tense; this was the moment of greatest danger. The men were like dancers, each following the familiar pattern of movements that was special to them. A few sparks rose and flared as the golden stream flowed. A tiny drop of molten steel splashed on to the stone flagged floor, close to Ben's feet. He flinched as it exploded up towards his face, missing his eye by inches. One false move, one slip of the elbow and they'd have white hot metal swilling round their boots. Another drop splashed down on to the floor, and Ben could not help but gasp as it jumped up and landed red and spitting on the wet rags that covered the melter's arm.

"Look out!" Ben cried. "Look out!"

"Shurrup!" the puller-out snapped.

Ben stared in amazement as the melter calmly finished the pouring, ignoring the hissing and burning that rose from his arm. At last the metal was poured. The melter set down the crucible pot. He flicked the burning spatter of steel to the floor and the men stood back as he went fast to dunk his arm in the water trough. Ben followed him, white-faced.

"Are tha burnt?" he asked.

The melter grinned and swung his scorched arm back and forth, easing his shoulder. "Nay lad. I got a bit warm though."

The puller-out came after them. "Daft little bugger!" he said. "Could have caused a right spill, yelling like that."

"He'll learn," said the melter kindly. "Can't stop when we're pouring, lad. Can't stop for anything. 'Cept of course, if a bonnet's off."

"Bonnet?"

"Aye. It's most unlikely. Specially with a grand potman like your dad. But if you ever hear the cry . . . 'Bonnet's off!' Then you get the hell out'a there."

Ben's legs had suddenly gone all wobbly and he sat down on the bottom step outside the workshop. He looked up to see that the packing women had stopped their work and were shouting excitedly at each other. Jack Carter pushed his way through them and strode towards the puller-out.

"Bad news!" he cried. "Bad news! Poor Samuel's back in Sheffield."

The men stared at him, not understanding.

"Samuel . . . the Chartist. They've brought him back from York in a great black cart and taken him to his wife."

Ben turned around on the steps, open mouthed. The puller-out pushed past him, all spills forgotten.

"Holberry?" he growled. "Does tha mean that he's dead?"

"Aye," the carter cried, red-faced with excitement. "They've brought him back in a coffin. He's to be buried tomorrow. All the town shall go."

As the news spread through the Works, the high whine of the grinding wheels stopped, one by one. Even the water wheel was brought to a standstill and the great tilt hammer silenced. The men came out into the yard, speaking low, their faces solemn.

"Who is it?" Ruth whispered. "Who is it that's dead?"

"Samuel Holberry," her mother told her. "The Chartist. You were too young to take much notice, love, he planned a rebellion two years back. All us workers in the north were to take over the town halls."

"Our Maggie and Joe were right upset," said Ben. "Our Maggie was friends with his wife."

39

"That's right," said Jess. "Poor Mary Holberry were expecting a baby when it all happened. I've heard since that the poor bairn were born sickly; didn't live long. Not surprising really. They arrested Mary, along with Samuel. Locked her up all alone for two days, wanting her to tell them what the Chartists had been planning. She said nothing of course and they had to let her go in the end."

"Poor thing," said Ruth. "Perhaps she knew nowt about it."

Jess laughed. "Oh, I think she knew all right. It were quite a thing those Chartists planned you know. Nottingham was to join in," said Jess, "and Barnsley and Bradford and some of those towns up north near Newcastle. It never happened, of course. He were betrayed." Jess sighed. "Really, he were mad to try. I can't see as they ever stood a chance. They put him on the treadmill in Northallerton gaol. I reckon that's what's killed him. He were still a young man, you know. Can't have been more than twenty seven."

"Death sentence!" the puller-out spoke with anger. "Death sentence. That's what it was."

The workers went quiet as the door to the counting house flew open. The clerk strode out, followed by Mr Dyson. All that could be heard was the grunting of pigs from the sty by the Works' gates, and the cackle of fowls and geese.

"Well?" John Dyson asked. "What's up? Why have you stopped?"

There was a great deal of whispering, then one of the grinders told of Samuel Holberry's death.

"We'll get ourselves back to work now, Mr Dyson," he said. "But Sheffield workers are shutting up shop to follow his coffin tomorrow and we must do the same."

There were shouts of agreement. Mr Dyson looked annoyed.

"But our grinding wheel is just fixed," he said.

There was silence again. Then slowly they all shuffled back to their places, and the thud and whine of working sounds soon filled the valley once more.

"What will you do?" Nan asked as they sat down to their evening meal.

"We've agreed it all," Ben's dad told her. "There'll be no steel made in Abbeydale tomorrow. No . . . nor any pots, either. I shall go to the funeral and take Ben with me."

"Is the whole Works stopping then?"

Frank Sterndale nodded.

"Maybe I'll come too," said Nan. "They say the coffin shall be brought from Attercliffe. I could call in on our Maggie and sort out that baby for her."

"No, Mother," Ben's father was firm. "It's a day of respect for Samuel. There'll be no jobs done, and nobody taken to the Workhouse. You can have our Ben next Monday, it's always a quieter day at work."

Nan sighed, then she patted his hand. "You're right," she said. "I'll put on my best black and come with you, for though I think he was mad that Samuel were a brave lad. No doubt of that."

CHAPTER FIVE

A Chartist's Funeral

When wilt thou save the people?
Oh, God of Mercy, when?
Not kings and lords, but nations!
Not thrones and crowns, but men!

Ebenezer Elliott, The People's Anthem

BEN HAD NEVER seen Sheffield Town so crammed with people, all dressed in their Sunday best clothes. Shops were closed and the worksheds silent. Nan said no more about visiting Maggie.

The long slow-moving procession was led by the Female Chartists, singing as they went and carrying flags. The men followed and then came a fine brass band. Ben and his family joined the great mass of people who marched behind the coffin up to the General Cemetery. Jess and Ruth walked with them, and Ben glanced nervously at the stooped shoulders of the puller-out striding ahead of them, awkward in his clean dark suit.

They moved in an orderly procession, heads bowed in respect. The cobbled streets of Sheffield were filled with a great clattering that came from so many clogged feet.

Nan stared about her, bewildered. "I've never seen so many poor working folks all together," she said. "Where are they coming from? Look at them, all washed and brushed and sober."

"See there," said Jess, taking her daughter's arm. "See that poor lass. She's the one I'm sorry for."

She pointed out the pale young woman who walked far ahead of them behind her husband's coffin.

"They say she still stands by the Chartists. That must take some doing! The cause has lost her her husband and her child."

Nan was sweating, with the hot sun beating down on her black bonnet, and the closeness of the crowd. She dabbed at her forehead.

"Now that I see them, I seem to understand the lad better," she said. "They're decent hardworking folk and they've given up a day's wages to be here . . . them that's working. Why should they not have a vote? That's what Samuel wanted, didn't he?"

Frank Sterndale sighed. "Aye, that's the heart of it, Mother. He wanted a great deal more, but getting the vote for ordinary folk's the main thing. Just look at them! If all that's here had joined the lad in his rebellion, well . . . who knows what might have happened?"

Samuel Holberry was laid to rest with sorrow and respect; his fellow Chartist George Harney gave a stirring speech.

"We swear to have retribution for the death of Holberry; swear to have our Charter Law."

"Aye . . . aye." A great wave of agreement surged up from the crowd.

The journey home was quiet and thoughtful. Though the tramp of feet filled the streets there was little said and much to think about.

They stopped by the corn mill, almost halfway along the road that led out of Sheffield, along the bank of the River Sheaf.

"We'll wet our throats, and drink to Samuel and to the Chartists," said Frank Sterndale, pointing to the Robin Hood and Little John public house, close by the corn mill. Ben shrank back to let the puller-out go inside with his father.

It was late afternoon when they reached the Scythe Works.

"Hark at the quiet," Ben said as they turned the bend in the road and the Works came into sight.

It was strange indeed to have the great tilt hammers stilled at that time of day but, as they drew closer to the Works, it became clear that the workshops were not so still and not so quiet as they'd thought. A high grating whine came steadily from the grinding hull.

"Grinders at work?" Frank Sterndale said.

As they walked towards their cottage, they saw a gang of men gathering in the yard. Their voices were low but it was clear that they were angry.

Ben's father and old Joe glanced at each other. Without a word they went to join the gang. Ben followed behind with Nan and Jess.

"Who is it?"

"It's new grinders! Dyson's set on a couple of strangers. They don't belong to the Union! They pay no dues!"

"What right have they to take our work?"

"Have they been here all day?"

"Nay! There were no sign of them this morning."

"Elsie's old mother heard them. She can't get out of her bed, but *she* heard them."

"Aye. She says they started up as soon as we'd gone off to Sheffield, and they've worked since then."

"A *whole* day's wages they've been promised. That's what Betty said."

"Where's Dyson?"

"Not here."

"Where's Works' clerk?"

"Hiding in his office."

Suddenly there seemed to be agreement amongst the men. There were shouts of "Stop them . . . stop the traitors."

The men who usually worked in the grinding hull marched up to the doorway. The packing women followed and Ben was surprised that Jess hung back. Ruth clung to her mother's arm, looking frightened.

"It's all right," Ben told her. "They'll not really harm them."

Ruth shook her head. "Don't care if they do," she whispered. "It's just that I hate that grinding hull."

"It's her dad, you see," Jess told him. "We can't abide the place. You go in, Ben. Tell us what happens for it sickens me that Dyson should go against the Union's rules like this. Don't grinders have enough troubles without these fellows taking their jobs?"

Ben felt stupid. He should have remembered that Ruth's father had been killed in that same grinding hull. It must be almost five years since it had happened but, even though he'd been so small, Ben could remember the shock and the sadness of it. No wonder they couldn't bear to step inside the place.

"Go on," Jess smiled and pushed him. "Tell us what's done."

Ben squeezed in beside his father just in time to see one of the regular grinders pulling off the broad leather wheel bands that joined the grinding stones to the big drum.

The hiss of metal on stone ceased.

The strangers sat astride big wooden saddles, hanging forwards at their work over the watertroughs and grindstones. With panic and fear written on their faces, they stared at the sight of so many angry folk crowding into the cluttered grinding hull. They need not have been so fearful for the workers did nothing more than stand there amongst the piles of wheelswarf. They stood in stony silence. The frightened men clambered down shakily from their wooden saddles and ran.

Anger turned to smiles as they scurried like rabbits from the grinding hull.

"Hey . . . tha's left tha jacket!" Elsie cried. "Left their snap tins, too."

Ben's father was quiet that night as they sat at supper.

"Jess wouldn't go into the grinding hull," Ben said.

"No, she'll not set foot in there," said Frank.

"I can't remember what happened," Ben insisted. "I know her man was killed, but what happened to him?"

"Oh, don't ask, don't ask!" Nan shook her head.

Ben's father put down his spoon, his face drawn. "A terrible death," he said. "It doesn't happen often, mind, but when it does . . . well, nobody can do ought about it. The grinding stone exploded in his face."

Ben shuddered and felt suddenly sick. He wished he'd never asked. "No wonder," he said. "No wonder Jess would not follow you inside."

"Aye," his father sighed. "She's a good lass is Jess and fearless as they come, but she can't abide sight nor sound of that grinding hull."

They sat on in silence, then at last Nan spoke.

"Are you worried, Frank? Are you worried what Dyson might do?"

"Nay, Mother," he shook his head. "If Dyson has any sense he'll say nowt and we'll all be back at work tomorrow."

Nan shook her head. "I can't get over all those people," she said. "I've never seen anything like it."

Frank smiled. "I know what you mean," he said. "It's been a day of mourning, yet it's somehow made me hopeful. I've talked to old Joe and he agrees with me. First chance we get, we're going into Sheffield to see that George Harney. We're going to join the Chartists."

"Are you?" said Nan. "I hope you know what you're about."

CHAPTER SIX

The Grinder's Child

There draws the Grinder his laborious breath;
There, coughing at his deadly trade he bends;
Born to die young, he fears nor man nor death.

Ebenezer Elliott

B EN'S FATHER had been right. Mr Dyson said nothing.
The new grinders turned up the following morning,
looking nervous. It seemed they'd been taken on for
good, alongside the Union men. Work started as usual, the fast
hammer banging away at full tilt. There was much shaking of
heads in the melting shop.

"He's keen enough to use the Thorpes' wheel when his own
won't turn," said old Joe. "Then he brings in strangers at the
first chance. No wonder the grinders are angry. The Union
won't stand for it. They're all off to Sheffield tonight to see
what their mates have to say. I gather Jess's going, too!"

"Huh!" said the melter. "They'll not like that! A woman
meddling in Union business!"

The puller-out cracked out laughing. "You know our Jess!
They'll have a job stopping her."

Nan insisted on Ben having a day off work the following
Monday to help her carry bundles of baby linen into Sheffield
for his sister.

48

When Maggie married a fork grinder, Frank Sterndale had been very much against it. John's job was known to be the most dangerous of all the trades. "Do you want to be widowed before you're forty?" he asked.

But Maggie had been determined; John was the man for her. Now she struggled bravely with her growing family and John's ill-health.

Monday was always a quiet day for many of the craftsmen called it St Monday, and spent it recovering from the weekend's drinking. Ben was glad when Monday came round for a day away from the melting shop would be a real treat. A few months ago he'd have pulled a face at having to make the long trail from Abbeydale to Sheffield Town, loaded up with Maggie's bits and pieces.

"Nan . . . can't we go in the carrier's cart?" he begged, knowing well what the reply would be.

"What! Pay good money when we've two strong legs! Certainly not. Don't know what young lads are coming to these days. Carrier's cart indeed!"

They took the bendy road that ran alongside the River Sheaf. Nan was dressed in her best clothes, most respectable in her black gown and bonnet. She'd insisted that Ben put on his Sunday suit.

She clipped his ear to make him stand still while she combed his hair. "We'll not have them looking down on us in that Workhouse," she snapped.

"Are you scared they'll take me, too?" Ben giggled.

Nan clipped him again. "Don't you dare joke about such a thing."

They passed the Corn Mill and stared at the fine new houses that had been built up on the bankside, looking down over the River Sheaf.

"You'd have to be rich to live in them," Ben said.

Nan shrugged her shoulders. "Oh aye, there's plenty of money being made these days – for some!"

They could see where trees had been felled and lovely gardens planted. A maid was beating carpets round at the side.

It was almost noon by the time they arrived in Sheffield. They passed the wheel close to the River Sheaf where John worked. Fork grinding was lighter work than the wet scythe grinding that went on at Dyson's, but everyone hated the foul dry dust it produced.

"Pull up tha neckerchief and cover tha nose," Nan insisted. "Just while we get past."

Ben willingly obeyed. Thick clouds of dust with fine motes of steel in it puthered from the windows. The long upstairs room was the workplace for ten dry grinders.

"It makes you choke from right out here," Ben spluttered.

Even the high whine of metal on the turning grindstones could not cover the harsh sounds of the men coughing.

Nan shook her head, her eyes watering. "Why our Maggie had to wed a grinder, I'll never know. There's lads as young as you up there, breathing in all that muck."

"Apprentices?" said Ben.

"Aye. John told me they've a young lad your age, been working there since he was eight. Got the most dreadful cough, poor little fellow."

Ben shuddered. "I think I'm glad to be a cellar lad."

When they arrived at Maggie's house, they found her upset and flustered because she couldn't find the young child that they were to take to the Workhouse. Her face was red and sweaty and her huge stomach made her look very different from the pretty big sister that Ben could just remember. She grimaced and rubbed her back.

"I swear the poor bairn knows there's summat up," she said. "He's a terrible handful and no mistake. Can't keep still, not for a moment and he bites our little Jacky whenever he gets the chance. Sinks his teeth right in, he does."

Nan made her sit down and set about brewing some tea, wiping the children's hands and faces as she went.

"Yesterday, we found he'd got back into his old house next door," Maggie said. "I'd not be surprised if he's managed it again. Could you pop in and have a look, our Ben? There's two new young men moved in . . . ever so kind they've been, but they'll be working now. They've given me the key in case he should do it again."

Ben took the key from his sister but he was puzzled.

"If it's locked, how could he . . .?"

Maggie shrugged her shoulders. "I don't know. The child seems to have some way of getting inside."

Ben was glad to get out of the crowded room. It was cramped with crying babies and the smell of cats, bread, dirty clothes and damp babies' napkins, strung up across the room to dry.

There was just one privy for each set of six small back-to-back houses and Ben wrinkled his nose as he crossed the yard. The smell was even worse out there. Anyone could see that the cesspit was overflowing, so that stinking brown sludge puddled the yard. He clamped his hand over his nose, stepping carefully; he certainly didn't want his decent clogs caked in that stuff. It was hard to believe that these houses were newer than their own solid stone-built cottage out at Dyson's Works.

"Thrown together!" That's what Ben's father always said about them. "Thrown together, just to make fast money."

Ben pushed the key into the lock of the next door. As he

stepped inside, he couldn't help thinking how different it was to his sister's home; so bare and quiet, though you could hear the faint sound of Maggie's voice through the wall. Someone had scrubbed it recently but it still didn't smell good, not like Nan's kitchen.

There was a table, two stools and a wooden bench-bed built into the thin wall that divided it off from Maggie's house. The bed was covered with old sacking.

Ben realised that he should have asked the boy's name.

"Boy!" he shouted awkwardly. "Boy! Are you there?"

He waited in the quietness and was just about to turn back when he thought he heard a faint shuffle and a giggle. Ben stared about him. The child couldn't be here and hiding, there was nowhere to hide. Then he thought he saw the sacking bedcover twitch just a bit. He smiled and caught the sound of a faint cough as he strode across the room and yanked off the worn sacking.

The child lay beneath the cover clutching a dirty rag to his chest. His eyes were tight shut as though asleep. Ben had expected a crawling baby. Though small and thin, this little chap must be at least two years old.

As Ben stared down at him, the corner of the boy's mouth twitched and again came the small suppressed cough. Ben had a quick flash of memory. He used to tease Nan when he was small by pretending to sleep.

"Come on," said Ben. "I know that trick."

One eye peeped open at him and quickly shut again. Suddenly the child leapt from the bed and dived underneath it, dragging the rag after him.

Ben blinked, stunned by the speed with which he'd moved.

"Come here," he shouted crossly, feeling that he was being made a fool of. He bent down and grabbed hold of one dirty bare foot.

Tiny sharp teeth sank into his hand.

Ben was so shocked that he let go. "You little devil," he cried.

Ben was having no nonsense now; he hurled himself under the bed just in time to see the boy's head and shoulders disappearing back into Maggie's house between two loose wooden boards.

"Ah . . . so that's how you do it," he said. "No wonder you don't need a key." He grabbed the boy's ankles roughly and hauled the child out from underneath the bed. It was easy enough to do for the tiny legs were thin as sticks.

The child screamed. "Dada!" he shouted, reaching for the dirty rag that he'd dropped, his small body shaking with the harsh coughing fit that came upon him.

"All right! All right!" said Ben. "You can have it, if you must." He picked up the smelly piece of stuff that felt like worn leather and gave it to the boy. The coughing ceased quickly, once the rag was returned.

"What's your name?"

The child stared up at him, his eyes watering. His hair was long and matted, and the worn smock that covered his thin body was dirty. "Boy," he muttered. "Boy, boy."

His anger gone, Ben crouched down beside him. The child was quiet enough now that he'd got his rag back. How could Maggie have let him get into this state? But then Ben remembered that Maggie couldn't manage at all and that was why they were here.

Ben took tight hold of the child's hand, fearing that he'd dash back under the bed at the slightest hint of trouble. He was surprised to find the small fingers curled trustingly round his own. Now, how was he to get him back to Maggie's. Ben frowned; then he suddenly smiled, remembering how crafty

Nan had been when he was little.

"It's dinnertime," said Ben.

"Dinner," the boy repeated, his face brightening.

"Yes. Dinnertime," said Ben. "Come to Maggie's house for your dinner."

The child meekly allowed himself to be taken back next door.

"Give him a bit of bread, will you, Maggie? I've told him it's dinnertime. It's the only way that I could fetch him."

Maggie stared in surprise at Ben, then she nodded. "Aye . . . I've a bit of bread and cheese. We can all have a bite to eat. You did well, Ben. He'll never come quietly like that for me. You should have heard him screaming when I dragged him out of there yesterday."

"What's his name?"

Maggie shrugged her shoulders. "We just call him . . . Will's boy. William Glossop's boy."

Ben was appalled. "You mean he's not even got a proper name?"

Maggie's eyes quickly filled with tears and her voice shook. "You don't know what it's been like," she said.

"Now don't take on," said Nan. "Ben meant nowt."

"It's been so hard," Maggie told them. "His poor dad so sick that he couldn't even speak, and me and John trying to keep them both alive, though we're struggling ourselves. He won't let me wash him, he won't let me comb or cut his hair. He's like a wild beast, though I must say it's not his fault."

"Hmm," said Nan. "Good thing we've come."

Ben watched as the child scurried off with his bread and cheese into the corner of the room. He gobbled it up like a starving cat, making small whimpering sounds.

"They'll want to know his name, up at the House," said Nan

firmly. "We'd best call him William after his father."

"Poor William did love him," said Maggie, her voice still shaky. "That's what makes me feel so bad about sending him away. That man worked on and on, even though he were so sick that he could hardly stand. He went into work two or three days a week, just to earn enough to keep the boy with him. Then at the end he could only manage one morning a week, to get bread for the child; he couldn't eat a thing himself. He dragged himself up to that grinding hull the very day he died. Our John had to carry him home."

Tears poured down her face, making Ben swallow very hard. Little William stared at them from the corner.

"He'll not be parted from that rag," said Maggie. "It's a filthy piece of his father's grinding apron, but he'll not sleep without it. He goes mad if you try to take it . . . raises hell. I couldn't do with that, so I cut it down a bit and let him keep it."

"Aye, well," said Nan. "I don't like the sound of that cough he's got, but they'll sort him out where he's going. We're doing the best thing for him. He'll be fed and kept clean up there and they'll give him some medicine. There's nobody that can see to him here and certainly not you. Now has he any other clothes? Let's get him sorted out."

"Yes," said Maggie, still sniffing. "I've washed a fresh smock for him."

CHAPTER SEVEN

The Workhouse

They mix our bread with bran,
They call potatoes bread;
And, get who may, or keep who can,
The starved, they say, are fed.

Ebenezer Elliott

B EN'S CLOGS clattered over the cobbles. He carried young
William piggy-back, for Nan had thought it the quickest
way for them to go. The child was no weight and he
clung on tightly, one arm wrapped round Ben's neck while the
other hand clutched his smelly rag. Sometimes it stuck into
Ben's ear, tickling and making him want to giggle. Ben liked
the feel of the small child on his back, even though that rag
stank. William stared about him wide-eyed at the sights and
sounds that filled the streets.

"See, he's quiet and good," said Ben.

"Aye," Nan agreed, with a chuckle. "His eyes are fair
popping. I daresay he's never been out of Grinder's Lane
before. Never seen a carriage and four, never seen a market
stall."

They walked along the river bank and stepped out on to the
scrubby piece of common land they called Mill Sands. The
child began to kick and whimper; Ben had all on to hold him.

"I think he wants to run," said Ben, swinging him down.

"Don't you dare let go of him," said Nan. "We'll see the last of him if you do. I know there's plenty of poor bairns that live on the streets, but this un's far too young."

"Come on, we'll both run," said Ben, snatching up the child's hand and lengthening his strides.

"Wun, wun," the boy cried, laughing with delight.

"Hold him tight," Nan shouted as they leapt over the tough stringy grass, dodging the prickly gorse bushes.

"Round the bush," Ben bellowed.

William yelled at the top of his lungs, ignoring the wild coughing that came with all the exertion. They hurtled along, the child's thin legs going like pistons.

Ben smiled to himself. This barefooted bairn could run like a hare. Ben would like to see him running through Ecclesall Woods. How he'd love it. The sun in his face, the sweeping branches catching at his hair. Suddenly the awfulness of what they were to do hit Ben like a brick. He slowed down, though the child pulled him onwards, still laughing and coughing.

"Boy wun," he cried, his eyes watering, two hectic pink spots on his cheeks.

Ben tried to calm him down. He was afraid that he'd made the child's cough worse, though it was clear that he loved the wild game. He has no idea, Ben thought. No idea where we are taking him.

For one stupid moment Ben wanted to let go of the small hand and yell at him to run right away. Run for his freedom . . . run for his life. But Ben was old enough and wise enough to know that that would never do. William could not last for more than a few days, living rough. He'd die of hunger and cold. Who could tell what harm he'd come to; he'd be terrified. No. Letting him go would be even worse than the Workhouse. There was only one hope, one possible hope. He turned around and watched the old lady who'd always looked after him, coming puffing and panting over the grass towards them.

"Nan?" he cried his face drawn with anxiety. He knew the enormity of what he must ask.

"It's all right for you," Nan grumbled, as she caught up with them. "All right for you on your strong young legs."

"Nan?" Ben cried, his eyes suddenly swimming.

"Whatever is it, lad?"

"Nan . . . do you think? Could we take him home with us?"

Nan said nothing at first. She pressed her lips together and looked away. Then she shook her head.

"Look at me, Ben," she said. "Look at me properly. I'm an old woman . . . really old. Now I see him, he's a bright little chap and I don't like it myself. But he's a wild one, anyone can tell that. I'm far too old to deal with him."

Ben sighed. She was right. His nan could never manage a fast-footed little rat like William, but in a way that made it all worse. Ben could see that the rules and restrictions of the

Workhouse would be hell to such a child. Ben thought back to his own young days. He'd never been spoilt or fussed, but there'd always been plenty of food, plenty of kindness from the workers, and above all there'd been the wonderful freedom of the woods.

"Nan, I could help. He could sleep with me up in the loft and I could see him washed and dressed before I go to work each day."

Nan shook her head. "You've got all on to get yourself to that workshop," she said. "Now let's be done with it and get ourselves back home."

The entrance to the Workhouse was grand with columns and steps in dressed Derbyshire stone, but the porter took them quickly across the yard, past the dreadful sounds of the Asylum block and into the Boys' School.

He knocked on a heavy wooden door and shouted out, "Two for the school."

"Oh no," Nan cried out angrily. "It's only one. This is my grandson. He's a fine cellar lad and earns his keep."

There was the chinking of keys from inside and three clanging bolts were drawn before the door swung open. A powerful smell of carbolic soap came wafting out.

The warden who opened the door was a fat, greasy-haired woman. She scowled impatiently at them.

"Now make up your mind. Is it one or two?" she demanded.

"It's just this little un," said Nan, pushing the child forward. "The poor bairn's an orphan."

William still clutched his scrap of grinding apron. He peeped down the dark corridor, then dodged back and grabbed tight hold of Ben's leg.

"All right, all right," said Ben.

"Infants' room. You'd best bring him in just while we take his name and details," the woman said.

The door had to be bolted again and locked behind them.

"This way," the woman told them. They followed her fast down a long corridor that was being scrubbed at the far end by two silent boys of about the same age as Ben. Faint cries and shouts could still be heard from the Asylum next door. They were taken into a small room with a desk and untidy sheaves of papers piled on shelves.

The woman opened a door on the far side. "One to be shorn and scrubbed, Matron," she said loudly.

"Here's a shirt that my granddaughter washed for him," Nan said, holding out the small bundle that Maggie had given her.

The woman sniffed. "Might as well keep it. There's only uniform worn here. Now then . . . what's his name?"

The other door swung open and the matron came in carrying a small gingham smock and a pair of scissors.

"This the one?" she nodded at William.

"Ye . . . es," Nan answered uncertainly.

"Is that him I can hear coughing?" the matron asked.

"Yes," said Nan. "I know it does sound bad, but a treacle posset should soothe him. Black treacle and milk is best, so I always say."

"Treacle? Milk? Linseed tea's what he'll get," said the matron. "Anyway I know that kind of cough. I doubt he'll be with us long! Grinder's child did you say?"

"Oh no!" Nan cried, quite distressed when she saw what the woman meant. "I'd think that a drop of good medicine and some nice warming liniment rubbed on his chest should do the trick."

"We've no time for pampering and special nursing," the matron insisted. "And that dirty thing'll have to be burnt!"

Before any of them had time to understand, she snatched the leather rag from William's hands.

"No!" Ben cried out.

Nan stepped back shaken at the sudden way the woman had swooped. William hurled himself after his rag like a mad dog, screaming and biting and coughing into the matron's face.

"Stop him," the warden shouted, dropping her pen. "Shall I fetch a stick to him?"

Ben could not bear it. He grabbed the rag back from the matron and put it into William's hands. William subsided at once, sobbing and cowering behind Ben, his eyes and nose running.

Nan, white faced and clearly shaken, put her hand on William's head. "You don't understand," she said. "It's his father's grinding apron, just a scrap of it. All the child has left of him. Seems to bring him a bit of comfort."

"We can't have any such thing in here." The matron angrily rubbed her hand where William's sharp teeth had caught her flesh. "It's against the rules and if he bites, he'll be beaten."

"Oh no he'll not," Nan answered calmly.

"If that child comes into the Workhouse he'll do as he's told," the warden wagged her finger at Nan. "This is a Workhouse, not a place for coddling brats. Good grief, we'd have the whole of Sheffield in here if we treated 'em soft."

Nan was shaking from head to toe. "That's why they'd rather starve in the streets than step in here," she cried.

The two women looked at each other with outrage.

"Are you leaving this brat here, or not?" the matron snapped.

Ben snatched William up into his arms. He was ready to run and could have yelled out loud with joy when he heard Nan's reply.

"I am not," she said. "He's coming home with me. I wouldn't leave a dog in this place."

"Wicked time wasters," the matron muttered. "Get rid of them." She opened the door that she'd come through and slammed it after her.

The other woman snatched up her keys. "Get out," she snapped.

Ben ran down the corridor with William in his arms. Nan followed as fast as she could, the angry warden marching after them. Ben had to stop at the door for it was locked. He would not put William down for fear of him being snatched away again. The woman unlocked the door in silent rage, she would not even look at them.

Once outside, they walked fast and furious away, needing to put a good distance between themselves and the hateful place. William was very quiet, trotting along beside Ben, clutching on to his sleeve. At last Nan stopped. She was finding it hard to catch her breath and Ben saw that her hand was pressed to her side as though in pain.

"Sit down a minute, Nan," he said. "Look, there's the Pond Well, just ahead. I'll bring you a sip of water."

"Oh Ben," she said gasping, tears filling her eyes. "What ever have we gone and done?"

CHAPTER EIGHT

A Good Little Chap

Again a child, where childhood rov'd I run;
While groups of speedwell, with their bright blue eyes,
Like happy children, cluster in the sun.

Ebenezer Elliott

IT WAS BEGINNING to get dark when they reached the Scythe Works. Ben carried William on his back; the child had walked until he was dropping.

"Why bless him," said Nan. "I swear he's fallen fast asleep."

Ben laughed. "I can tell. He's gone all warm and floppy. His breath is tickling my neck."

Nan sighed. "I don't know what your father's going to say."

They found Frank Sterndale sitting at the table in his dusty work clothes, lighting a candle. He'd got a small fire burning in the grate. "Ah, there you are," he said. "I was wondering if I was to get any supper tonight."

Ben and his grandmother came in sheepishly, saying nothing and looking a little awkward.

"Now then, son, what's that you've got there?"

Nan took the sleeping child gently from Ben's back. She set him down carefully on the soft rag rug in front of the fire.

Frank Sterndale got up from his chair, staring from her to William in amazement. Then he sat down again with a bit of a thump and scratched his head. "Eh Mother, what have you done?"

Nan shook her head. "God help me," she said. "That Workhouse is worse than I feared, Frank. I couldn't leave him there and that's that. We shall have to eat porridge tonight."

Nan went to take off her bonnet, then she set about ladling oatmeal into a pot.

"I'm going to look after him," said Ben, wishing to reassure his father. "You see if I don't."

"Thee," Ben's father sighed and ruffled his son's hair. "Tha can't look after theesen yet. Still, I hate the thought of any poor child being put into the Workhouse. We shall have to think about it, Mother, it's you that should bear the greater burden. I must say he looks a good quiet little chap, sleeping there."

Ben and his nan looked at each other.

"Get yourself washed up, our Frank. This porridge shall be ready in a minute."

They ate their supper while William slept.

"Now," said Nan determinedly. "He's got to be bathed and that hair of his has got to be cut. My eyes may be bad, but I can see that it's crawling with lice."

"Hmm," Ben sighed. He didn't think that was going to be easy, but if he was to take William up to the loft to sleep with him as he'd promised, he'd rather the child was bathed and cleaned up first.

"Now, Frank, why don't you wander round to Widow Blackitt's," Nan suggested. "Get yourself a mug of ale and we'll have this little un sorted out by the time you come back."

Frank got up from his chair, smiling and surprised. "Good heavens, Mother, I shall have to send you down to that Workhouse more often. Don't worry, I'll be off before you change your mind."

Nan warmed up a bowlful of porridge and set a kettle of water to boil. "You'd best wake him," she told Ben. "We've a lot to do."

William was calm enough at first. Ben could see that he was sleepy and puzzled by his surroundings, but the warm fire and porridge seemed to cheer him. He ate greedily, scooping up the porridge with filthy hands.

"Eh dear," said Nan, watching him. "We've a long way to go and no mistake."

Ben dragged the tin bath up from the cellar and set it in front of the fire. William watched suspiciously, but he didn't stop eating. It was when Nan poured the first lot of steaming water from the kettle that he dropped the bowl and dived beneath the wooden settle.

Nan calmly set another kettle to boil. "We're going to have to have a think about this," she said. "What if you stripped off and got in . . . maybe then he'd be more willing."

"What?" Ben stared at her. He hadn't stripped off in front of Nan for a year or so. She usually went off to bed and left him and his father to bathe themselves in private.

"Now look," said Nan. "You wanted him here. You begged me to have him. You're going to have to do it my way or not at all. I can't do with a wild rumpus in my kitchen. You'll strip yourself off as I say . . . and what's more, you'll have a haircut, too."

Ben sighed. Bringing William home with them wasn't going to be an easy thing, he could see that.

"All right," he said. "What do you want me to do?"

"Fetch the scissors and sit down here."

Nan set about Ben's hair with an alarming snipping sound. "Don't make me bald," he begged.

"Course I won't," Nan whispered. "Hardly taking anything

off. Just ignore the bairn and smile as though you're enjoying it."

Ben felt foolish, but he could understand Nan's crafty way of thinking, so he sat there grinning stupidly as she snipped her scissors round his head.

Nan started to sing in her croaky old voice.

"Don't cry my darling,
Don't cry my little lamb,
Snip his bonny hair away.
And turn him into a man."

Ben had a job not to burst out giggling, but two small dusty hands appeared from beneath the settle, still clutching the dirty rag. William peeped out at them curiously.

Ben stuffed his fist into his mouth to stop himself from laughing out loud. "It's working," he breathed.

William crept out, his mouth wide open with amazement.

"Take no notice," whispered Nan.

In a moment William was upright and standing trustingly beside Ben, watching the snipping scissors.

"Snip, snip, snip," sang Nan, and suddenly the scissors bit through a good sized tuft of Ben's wirey brown hair. She thrust the small handful of curls into William's face.

"Hey," said Ben.

"Smile," hissed Nan.

William snatched up the hair and sniffed at it. He laughed as it tickled his nose. " 'Nip, 'nip, 'nip," he cried.

"Snip," said Nan, and she clipped a good sized tuft from the front of William's matted curls. He looked rather surprised and uncertain, his chin trembling.

"Oh heck," Ben whispered as Nan returned to his own hair. "Now you've done it."

"No. Boy . . . 'nip Boy," said William pulling at the curls on the top of his own head.

"You're a sly old woman," said Ben.

"I've had to be, to raise you," Nan told him.

"All right, all right," Ben soothed as he bent forward and lifted William up on to his knee. He held him firmly in place while Nan clipped quickly and matted dark straw-coloured locks fell to the ground.

" 'Nip, 'nip, 'nip," said William.

Ben and Nan were pleased with themselves. They'd managed to get William into the bath tub without mishap. Ben had taken off his own shirt, then William's. He pulled off his own breeches, then hopped quickly into the water without looking at Nan. William had willingly followed him, though it seemed the leather rag must go into the bath, too.

"Best thing," said Nan. "It needs a good wash as much as he does."

It had been very cramped with them both in the tub, so Ben had soaped himself quickly and got out. Now the child crouched still in the water, his eyes wide and anxious as Nan soaped first his shorn head and then his rag.

"Good lad, good lad . . . that's my boy," she murmured.

Ben watched them dreamily, remembering that it had been like this when he was small. It was going to be all right; he was sure of it. Nan was old, but she was kind and crafty. She knew how to do it.

"You were right," he said. "We've to think it out . . . not scare him."

"Aye," said Nan. "He's a good little chap really."

Ben pulled his breeches on, then crouched down by the bath tub, blowing gently on the water so that a tiny wave tickled William's stomach. The worried look fled and a faint smile touched the corners of his mouth. Ben blew again and William laughed, swishing at the water with his hands.

"Waves," said Ben. "Little waves. See, he likes it."

"Wabes," said William. He swished the water down towards his toes, giggling now.

"Steady on," said Nan as a bigger wave of soapy water swung from one end of the tub to the other.

"Wabes!" William yelled. Water slopped over the edge of the tub, giving Nan's rag rug a good soaking.

"Stop it," Nan shouted. "That's enough! Grab him, Ben!"

Ben dived at William, but he was too late. William got to his feet in sudden panic, taking a great rush of water with him. He leapt from the tub terrified, catching the edge with his foot. The tub rocked and tipped. William screamed and dived beneath the settle as Ben set it to rights.

It was just then that Frank Sterndale came back, to find the kitchen swilling with water and his mother shouting at Ben, face all red, skirts clutched up above her knees.

"Good grief!" he cried. "What the bloody hell's going on here?"

It had taken a bit of effort to sort out the mess. Ben's father set to with the yard brush, swilling water out of the back door, while Nan and Ben hung the rugs and cloths up to dry by the fire. It had taken a good deal of patience to coax William out from his hiding place. Ben's father squeezed the water out of the newly-washed leather rag thoroughly and at last the sight of it all clean and steaming and willingly offered back, tempted him out from beneath the settle. Nan rubbed a little of her own liniment on his chest so that he smelt sweetly of camphorated oil and cloves. They dressed him in a fresh, warmed smock and gave him the promised warm posset of black treacle and milk.

"Sip it," Nan insisted. But it was clear from the way William guzzled it down and licked his lips that he thought it much too good for sipping.

Wearily Ben led him up the loft ladder, carrying a candle. He lay down beside him on the straw-stuffed mattress to show him how they were to sleep. There was just about room for two. They covered themselves up snugly with one of Nan's soft woven rugs. William wriggled about for a while, then lay still, staring wide-eyed up into the rafters where the candlelight threw dark shivering shadows on the roof. At last the slow sounds of his breathing told Ben that he slept, still clutching his rag.

Ben snuggled down beside the warm sleeping child, sniffing the faint familiar smell of camphor. He gently stroked the shorn head that was now clean and soft, the colour of rabbit's fur. Ben rolled over and pulled out his Chartist's pamphlet from beneath the mattress. He stared at it for a moment, the letters dancing up and down in the candlelight. It had been a long day, even though he hadn't gone to work. He let it fall to the floor unread. A gentle snore came from William's throat. Ben smiled and blew out the candle.

CHAPTER NINE

Mary Ann

'Tis passing sweet to wander, free as air,
Blythe truants in the bright and breeze bless'd day.

Ebenezer Elliott

WILLIAM wriggled and whimpered in his sleep. Ben found it hard to settle down. In the early hours he became very restless; something warm and damp was creeping beneath him. His eyes flew open. William had wet the mattress, though he still snored happily. Ben leapt up from the bed disgusted, ready to wake his father and Nan. He was halfway down the ladder when he stopped. He knew that Nan must be very tired after the day they'd had; he could hear her muttering in her sleep. What good would it do to wake her up? Didn't she need her sleep more than ever now there was William to see to?

"Should have fetched the chamber pot," he muttered to himself.

Ben went to get the chamber pot from the cupboard in the kitchen. Then he climbed back up the ladder and wearily rummaged in the linen chest for dry clothes to spread beneath them both. William slumbered on, even when Ben gently lifted him. At last Ben lay back, comfortable again, but wrinkling his nose at the close smell of urine. His cosy loft would soon be stinking like Maggie's home. He was still tired when his father woke him in the morning.

Ben dressed himself and then woke William, who rolled over on the mattress, staring about him fearful and puzzled.

"Come on," Ben told him. "We've got to get washed."

William shook his head. He clearly thought he was quite washed enough from last night.

"Look," said Ben. "Wet. You've made my mattress wet and smelly. Should use the pot, or I'll have to tie babby's clouts round you."

William shuffled backwards, still shaking his head. It was clear he'd have dived beneath the bed if it had been anything other than a straw pallet laid on the floorboards.

Ben frowned, then he suddenly remembered what to do.

"Dinner," he said cheerfully.

"Dinner," said William. He stood up shakily, and offered Ben his hand.

William was sitting quietly at the table, when Ben and his father left for work. He'd polished off one bowl of porridge, scooping it up with his hands, and was happily starting on a second bowl while Nan made great show of using her spoon.

Frank Sterndale shook his head. "As if we haven't troubles enough," he said.

Ben forgot about William once he was back in the crucible workshop. The puller-out was in an angry and excitable mood, muttering the name 'Mary Ann' over and over again, in between barking orders. Ben was soon breathless with running up and down the stairs, back and forth with buckets of ale.

"I think he's fallen out with his wife," Ben told Widow Blackitt. "He'll do nowt but bellow her name."

"Why!" said Widow Blackitt. "His wife's been dead these twenty years."

"Well, he does nowt but grumble on about Mary Ann. I thought he were too old to go chasing after women."

"Ah," Widow Blackitt's fat cheeks trembled with amusement. "Mary Ann is it? Why you dafty, Mary Ann's no wife to him, nor to any man."

"Who is she, then?"

But Widow Blackitt would only shake her head. "I'm saying nowt," she said. "Ask your father."

And though he tried his hardest, Ben could not get her to say a word more about the mysterious Mary Ann.

As soon as he was back in Dyson's Yard, Ben smelt trouble. The packers seemed to be in uproar, some laughing, some screaming. Fowls and geese squawked and flapped in all directions.

"Ben . . . catch him, Ben," Nan's voice croaked.

And suddenly a panting breathless little body came whirling and coughing towards Ben, flinging itself at him, knocking his buckets of ale sideways, so that half the contents slopped out on to the yard.

Ben staggered backwards trying to keep his feet, and Jess snatched up the kicking, screaming William. He turned to bite her hand, but Jess was too quick for him and pulled his hands behind his back. "Ah no you don't," she said. "I'm wise to that little trick, my lad."

"We can't have this." Frank Sterndale stood at the top of the stone steps, up to his elbows in grey clay. "They're splashing burning steel all over their boots in here. Haven't we danger enough without a barmy bairn running wild. I'm sorry, Mother, but he'll have to go."

Nan came panting up to Jess and took William from her.

"I don't know," she said, her face was red and pouring with

sweat. "He's good as gold one minute and like a mad beast the next. I can't seem to keep him inside . . . he wants to be out."

"I'm sorry, Ben," Frank Sterndale said coming slowly down the steps to them. "We've tried our best, but Dyson's is not the place for him."

Ben stared down at William, remembering the sleepless night, and the mess and smell. It would be easier to send him back to the Workhouse, but they'd maybe beat him; he'd certainly never run wild again. Then Ben remembered the woods and how, in his mind's eye, he'd seen the child running free.

"Let me take him in the woods," he said.

"The woods?" His father stared at him.

"Aye. Remember how I used to run and run in there. If he can be free in the woods, then maybe he'll be quiet when he's at home."

"Aye," said Ruth, coming to his aid. "I'm sure that'd help. Can't you remember how me and Ben went every day to see the charcoal burners? We ran like dogs, and wore ourselves out."

"You've a job of work to do," Ben's father told him.

"I could take him in the woods while they're eating their dinner," Ben said hopelessly. He knew that was ridiculous, for he barely got ten minutes to gobble a bit of bread and cheese in the middle of the day while there was a quiet moment.

"Where's that lad wi'the ale," old Joe snarled down at them from the top of the steps.

Ben groaned inwardly. No doubt he'd have something to say about Ben shirking his work. Then the melter appeared beside him. Frank Sterndale went over to them both and they all had a moment's quiet talk. The puller-out spat and Ben was sure that he heard him speak the name of Mary Ann again.

"Aye. We'll give 'em an hour," the melter said. "Dyson's not about today. Let them know in the grinding hull. They want their meeting, let them have it now."

So, suddenly and very surprisingly William was handed over to Ben, and he was told that they could have an hour in the woods but must not be late back.

"I wish I could go wi'them," Ruth sighed.

"Go on," said Jess. "There'll not be much packing done, for I'm going to have my say if there's talk of Mary Ann."

It was a long time since Ben had been in the woods with Ruth and he felt awkward, though he was grateful for the way she'd spoken up for him. She'd understood what he meant straight away.

"Here you hold one of his hands, I'll have the other," said Ruth. She seemed to be taking charge.

They crossed the cart track with William jumping and swinging happily between them, but as soon as they passed beneath the leafy canopy of the trees, he grew quiet and wide-eyed. He clung tightly to their hands, jumping nervously at the swish of ferns and the crackle of twigs beneath their feet.

"Oh dear," said Ben. "He's got that scared look again. I thought he'd want to run. I thought he'd go mad and wear himself out."

"It'll be all right," Ruth told him. "I bet he's never been in a wood before. He'll get used to it. We should run with him a bit . . . show him what fun it can be."

So they started to trot slowly along the soft wide path of trampled earth, giggling with foolishness. A great daft lad and lass, old enough to be workers, running as though they were bairns. The woods were carpeted with wild bluebells as far as the eye could see.

"Look at them!" Ruth shrieked. "Just smell them bonny

flowers."

The more they laughed, the more they shouted, the happier William grew, turning his face from one to the other until at last all three of them were running at full pelt and yelling as they leapt over stones and clumps of grass and fallen logs.

They slowed down as they reached one of the fast-running streams.

"He could paddle," Ruth gasped.

"Yes," said Ben. "Look William . . . water!"

William pulled back suddenly. "No," he cried. "Boy no wash."

Ben remembered the tipping bath tub and laughed. "Not for washing," he said, "just for fun. Watch me!" He kicked off his clogs and paddled into the middle of the stream.

Ruth hitched up her skirt and followed him. "Lovely," she cried. "Cool and tickly." She set to splashing water over Ben's trousers.

"I'll get thee!" he said.

William teetered on the edge of the pool, watching them open-mouthed. At last he dipped his toe in and almost toppled over with surprise. They both lunged across the stream to catch his hands again. After a moment of doubt, William was soon splashing along with them. He continued long after Ruth and Ben had staggered out of the water and thrown themselves down on the thick short mossy grass that surrounded the stream.

"This is better than work," said Ben.

"Yes," Ruth sighed. "I love the woods so much at this time of year. Look up at those fresh green leaves, all yellow and golden in the sun. In a few weeks' time they'll have darkened, and we'll have missed it all. It's nowt but work these days. I doubt they'll be letting us come again."

"Aye," said Ben. "I can't work out what's up wi'them today. And who's this Mary Ann?"

Ruth shook her head. "Mam won't tell me, though I've asked her time and time again. She says it's safer not to know. But this I can say. It's all got something to do with the new grinders that Dyson brought in. My mam won't keep her nose out of it. Some of the grinders tell her that it's men's business, but Mam can't let it rest. She says that the Grinders' Union *is* her business. Without their help we'd have starved when my father died. It was the Union men that found Mam her job at Dyson's."

"Aah," said Ben sympathetically. "So this Mary Ann has got something to do with the Grinders' Union?"

"I think so," Ruth nodded. "Mam gets very angry about it all. She says it's bad enough being a grinder – what with the danger and sickness – without your master setting non-Union men to work at your side and take your jobs. She says 'if Dyson don't change his ways soon, Mary Ann will have to make a visit.'"

Ben frowned. He couldn't work it all out. Suddenly they heard the distant sound of the tilt hammer thundering into life.

"We're late!" Ruth jumped to her feet. "We should be back."

Ben leapt up and into the water.

"Where's the bairn?" he shouted. He'd forgotten William while they talked. There was no sign of him near the stream.

CHAPTER TEN

The Book-Fuddler

B EN SCRAMBLED through the water and out on to the path.

"Is he there?" Ruth yelled.

"Yes, I can see wet footprints!" Ben set off fast, following the small damp marks. Ruth ran after him, grumbling. All the joys of running through the woods had gone.

"There!" he yelled and pointed as he caught sight of a bobbing head in the distance.

Though they chased him as fast as they could, William managed to stay just ahead of them. He was giggling as though he thought it a fine game. At last he stumbled out into the charcoal burners' clearing, stopping suddenly, scared by the sight of the burning woodstacks and soot-blackened men.

"Catch him!" Ben bellowed. "Get 'im will yer?"

William screamed as Green Mort swooped and picked him up. "What have we here? What a little rascal! I didn't think you'd a brother, Ben!"

"No, I haven't," Ben growled, panting into the clearing. "He's more trouble than any brother, I swear he is."

Ben and Ruth explained about William, complaining bitterly that he'd made them late and they'd be in trouble.

"My dad will send him back to the Workhouse," Ben told them.

The Book-Fuddler closed the book he'd been reading and strode long-legged across the clearing to join them. He took William from Mort's arms. "Let's have a look at him," he said.

William had gone very quiet and still, staring fearfully from one sooty face to the other.

The Book-Fuddler smiled sadly. "Ey dear, I'd rather see him living rough with us here in the woods than locked up in one of those bastilles. What do you say, Mort?"

Mort stroked William's shorn head. "Aye. He's a grand little ruffian I must say, and I miss my little uns bitterly. But what would we do with him, come winter? My missus'd not thank me to return with another mouth to feed."

"Hey! He's living wi'me," Ben cried. He'd not have William snatched away from him like that. "Hand him over. I've not given up on him yet."

Mort laughed and slapped Ben on the back. "Well, lad, I think you *have* found yourself a brother. You keep him if you can, but remember this – Dan Book-Fuddler and Mort is willing to give a bit of help."

SCYTHE-GRINDING.

It was mid afternoon by the time they got back to Dyson's Yard and work was in full swing, the slower plating hammer thumping steadily. William seemed calm enough, so they left him with Nan. The puller-out clouted Ben's ear and sent him running straight down to the cellar to rake out the hearths to build up the heat.

Ben's father did not roar or shout at their lateness; what he did was much worse. He left his pots and came down to the cellar, speaking firm and sorrowful.

"Next Saturday," he said wagging his finger at Ben. "Next Saturday you take him back to that House. We've other things to worry about than him."

Ben worked hard for the rest of the day, harder than usual if that were possible, but when at last the men were packing up for the day, he crept down to the potshop and hunted amongst the scraps for bits of soft clay.

"This'll keep him busy," he told his father hopefully. "I used to make clay mice and birds when I were little. Can you remember? It kept me good and quiet."

His father shook his head. "Next Saturday," he said.

When they got back to the cottage they found Nan sitting by a dying fire, the stew uncooked, the small room strewn with threads and cotton reels; wet smelly puddles on the floor. William was curled up on Nan's lap still clutching his rag; they were both fast asleep.

They all helped to get the fire built up and the supper cooked. Nan was grumpy, though thankfully William watched them quietly from beneath the settle.

They ate their meal in silence and Ben's father stood up as soon as he'd finished and told them he was off to Widow Blackitt's.

"Again?" said Nan. It was not like him to spend so much time drinking. Frank Sterndale was no fuddler.

"Why? You told me to go there last night," he snapped. "Am I not master in my own home?"

Nan shrugged her shoulders, surprised at his anger. He went out of the house without another word.

When they'd cleared the table, Ben covered it with oilcloth and brought out the clay. William had gone back to his hiding place beneath the settle, where he kicked at the wooden back board.

"Look," Ben told him. "You can make mice."

William frowned and kicked again.

"You get on with it," Nan advised. "Ignore him."

So Ben deftly produced a small clay mouse with a pointed nose, flat ears and a thin rolled tail. He made it run along the edge of the table squeaking.

"Now I'll make another," he announced.

But before he'd managed to finish it a small hand snatched up the first mouse. William sniffed at the clay creature, licked its head and came to stand at Ben's side.

"Boy do it," he said.

Ben smiled and nodded to Nan when he saw that the rag was left behind underneath the settle.

They'd made six clay mice between them when Nan said that it was time they got William off to bed. He went willingly enough, dosed up with Nan's special cough syrup, though he insisted on taking the mice with him and lining them up beside the mattress.

He was puzzled when Ben carried up the chamber pot.

"I don't like my mattress wet," Ben told him.

William grinned and rolled about on the bed.

"No," said Ben. "You have to use the chamber pot first. Use

it now before you get in."

William giggled and hid his head under the bed cover.

Ben sighed. "Watch me," he said.

William sat up in bed and watched with interest as Ben peed into the chamber pot.

"Now you!" he told him firmly.

William rolled off the mattress and cheerfully copied Ben.

"Yes," said Ben, delighted with his success. "You're a good boy."

When Ben came down from the loft he found Nan sitting by the fire, sighing and wiping a tear from the corner of her eye.

"What is it, Nan?" he whispered.

"Nothing really," she shook her head. "Being foolish! Not like our Frank to speak harshly to his mother. Would you run down to Widow Blackitt's? Tell your father I'm sorry. He's a hardworking man and he has every right to a sup of ale."

"Course I'll go," said Ben, "if you really want."

Ben was surprised to find that Widow Blackitt's door was closed, though the night was warm. He was puzzled too at the quietness that surrounded the alehouse. On a warm evening like this the doors would usually stand wide open, so that the buzz of gossip and laughter could be heard all about. He frowned as he lifted the latch for he could hear just one voice speaking out clearly, followed by a chorus of agreement. The voice was familiar, though for a moment he could not quite think why. Then as he swung the door open he saw that it was Dan the Book-Fuddler. He was standing up on a box and reading from a newspaper while everyone in the crowded alehouse listened in hushed silence.

"This is the report of a sermon preached by a Methodist Minister in Newcastle," he said.

"We want no sermons," Widow Blackitt burst out laughing, shaking her fist teasingly at him.

"You'll want to hear this," the Book-Fuddler insisted. "The Reverend Stephens is another one to speak out against the Workhouse."

"Is he now?"

"Fancy that!"

"A man of God!"

The whole room fell quiet. Ben saw his father sitting in the corner with Jess. He pushed his way through to them.

"I've a message from Nan," he started.

"Hush lad," his father pulled him down beside him. "Here take a sip of ale."

The Book-Fuddler began again, his voice deep and clear. Ben remembered how impressively he'd read the inscription on the charcoal burner's grave, just as though he addressed a huge gathering and now it seemed he did.

"These are the minister's very words. 'The poor are not going to stand for this. I will say that sooner than split up wife and husband and father and son – sooner than put people into dungeons to be fed on watery soup – sooner than wife and daughter shall wear a prison dress – sooner than that – the whole of Newcastle ought to be and shall be one blaze of fire.' "

His voice rose and cheers broke out.

"Aye," they shouted, "and Sheffield too!"

"Sheffield too!"

Ben's mouth dropped open. He stared from the Book-Fuddler to his father's grim face. Had this reading been chosen on purpose? The charcoal burner did not even look their way, but entered into heated discussion with the Thorpe brothers and some of the grinders. Jess got up and strode over to join them.

"Come on, lad . . . I'm going home," Frank spoke sharply.

Ben followed his father, his head full of worrying thoughts. It was only when they reached the Scythe Works that he remembered Nan.

"I forgot," he said. "Nan sent me to tell you that she was sorry. She never meant to stop you having your ale."

Frank Sterndale was still for a moment, Ben could not see his father's face in the darkness or know if he was angry.

"She was quite upset," he said.

"Was she? Bless her!" Ben's father put his arm round his son's shoulders and hugged him. "She's a good woman is your nan," he said. "And you, Ben, are a fine son. Now listen here . . . you've no more need to worry about that little un. However hard it is, we'll keep him from that Workhouse. I swear it!"

"Thank you, Father!" Ben hugged his father back, but then he pulled away in doubt. "It's a hard job, looking after him," he said. "I almost wanted rid of him myself today!"

"Aye," his father agreed. "It's a hard job all right is bringing up young uns. Nobody knows that better than me, but we'll all do it together. Now let's get ourselves inside and soothe tha nan."

CHAPTER ELEVEN

Mary Ann's Visit

And cannot the loud hammer, which supplies,
Food for the blacksmith's rosy children, make
Sweet music to thy heart?

Ebenezer Elliott

B EN WOKE in the middle of the night. William was restless and clutching his rag, whimpering in his sleep. Ben shook him awake and persuaded him sleepily to use the chamber pot again.

William wormed his way straight back in beneath the cover, and was soon snoring. Ben decided to carry the chamber pot downstairs and empty it ready for the morning. Cold night air blew in as he lifted the latch and opened the back door. Ben didn't fancy the chilly stumble down the garden to the privy, so he threw the urine over Nan's cabbages. As he closed the door again, he jumped at a faint sound behind him. His father was up and standing there in his night shirt, but he wasn't watching Ben; he was peering out of the front window into Dyson's Yard.

"Dad?" Ben whispered. "What's up?"

"Nowt, son . . . nowt. Just that I cannot sleep. You get off to bed."

Ben was puzzled, but he did as he was told. It was most unlike his father, for he was usually so exhausted by his work that he snored steadily all through the night.

Ben's father looked tired and distracted when they all sat down to their porridge. It was clear that he'd had a sleepless night and Ben wondered guiltily if it was worry about how they'd all manage with William that had caused it.

Nan began pulling out her wash tub and scrubbing board. "How I'm going to get all this done with that bairn beneath my feet, I don't know," she grumbled.

"Leave it, Nan," said Ben. "Do the washing another day."

"Huh!" said Nan sourly. "It's all very well for you to say that, but I missed my wash on Monday as you know, and we've not a clean scrap of clothing left."

Ben's father seemed to shake himself out of his daydream. "I'll not have you worn out, Mother. We'll take him into the potshop with us. I've managed with a bairn in my workshop when Ben were a tiddler, I can do it again. Set him treading clay . . . that'll sort him out!"

Ben smiled with relief. It seemed that his father had really meant it when he said he was determined that they should keep William.

"The charcoal burners will help us," he told them. "Mort says that he will keep an eye on him, if we take him into the woods."

"That's grand," his father said. "Just like old times, when he had you climbing trees and gathering berries for our dinner. Now you see, Mother, you are not to take it all on to yourself. There's folk willing to help and we must not be too proud to accept."

They gave William a lump of soft clay and set him up in a corner of the potshop. He seemed to settle happily to making mice.

"You can make little plates of peas," said Ben and showed

him how. William watched delighted with what Ben did.

"Dinner!" he cried.

"Yes, dinner," said Ben. "But you can't eat it!"

Ben had been mixing up the powdered clay with his father, when Cokey called him up to the melting shop to help stoke the furnace holes. It was only then that he realised that the Works were buzzing with whispers and tense excitement.

"What are they all on about?" he asked.

"Has tha not heard?" the cokey said. "Mary Ann has been in the night!"

Ben sighed. "Mary Ann again! Nobody will say who she is!"

Cokey laughed. "You don't want to know, lad! A proper written message has come, delivered to Dyson during the night. Clear warning to him. He must stop using these non-Union grinders, or else there'll be trouble."

Ben's mouth dropped again. "But who has sent it?"

"That's the mystery," Cokey winked. "It's signed, MARY ANN. We do not ask more."

When Ben was sent to fetch ale, he could not help but smile at the high spirits of the packing women.

"You should have seen Dyson's face," hissed Elsie. "Oh lor' it was a picture, but he said nowt!"

The great grin on Jess's face told what she thought about it; only Ruth looked miserable.

"I know about Mary Ann," he whispered to her.

Ruth turned very white and looked frantic.

"It's not even a person!" he said.

"Ah!" Ruth breathed. "It's a message you mean. Yes, I know that too, now."

Later that morning Ben was down in the cellar raking out the hearths when the most dreadful screaming started up. He dropped his bucket at once and ran up the stairs his legs shaking.

"What the devil?"

"What the heck?"

"Where's it coming from?"

"The potshop?"

"What's up?" asked Ben as he stumbled into his father's workshop.

William had backed himself into a corner of the potshop, screaming fit to wake the dead, his hands clapped over his ears. Frank Sterndale crouched before him, his face drawn with concern.

"What's wrong with him?" Ben asked.

"Damned if I can tell," said Frank. "He's happy as a pig in its trough one minute, then suddenly this! It seemed to be as soon as the hammer started up."

Ben stared amazed as William screamed and trembled, his head ducking up and down as each blow of the hammer sounded. "He's scared to bits. Can it really be the hammer?"

Ben had spent all his life within the sound of those hammers. It was hard for him to understand that it could cause such terror.

Frank scratched his head, scattering dried clay powder into his hair. "Aye. Look how he jumps at the sound of each blow and holds his ears. Maybe you should take him round to the forge and let him see what it's all about. He thinks the whole world is falling in on us when he hears that steeling hammer start up."

Ben laughed. "Devil's footsteps! Devil's thunderclaps!"

"Aye," said Frank, chuckling. "Something like that. You take him while the melting team are drinking their ale and not wanting thee. I'll see you right with them. Let him have a good look at what it is that makes such a racket. He'll see that it's not after him. Come on now little un! Nowt to be so scared about!"

Once soothed a little, William followed Ben willingly up the potshop steps and through the melting shop. He seemed happy to be out in the fresh air, but when Ben tried to take him down towards the tilt forge, he pulled back, crying again.

"Nowt to fear," said Ben. "I know, let's see the water first."

Ben steered him round the side of the great shed to where the water wheel turned steadily, taking water from the dammed-up river with a regular whooshing sound.

"Wash!" said William, hiccupping, his eyes now wide with interest.

"Yes. Big wash!" Ben agreed. "It turns the wheel and makes the hammer go. Makes big bangs; come and see."

William's fingers gripped tightly on to Ben's sleeve as they stepped down into the tilt forge. The heavy wooden shafts and cogs turned smoothly, with a gentle whirr and creak. The plating hammer was still but the great steeling hammer pounded up and down like the head of a giant flat-nosed dragon. Mr Price the forgemaster had it working at full tilt. It moved so fast that you could hardly see it go.

Ben found it hard not to giggle when he saw that William trembled from head to toe. He bent down, putting his arm around the thin shoulders.

"See," he said bellowing in William's ear and pointing. "It's banging away to make a scythe blade."

William watched open-mouthed, blinking and flinching at each drop of the hammer.

The forgemaster sat on a swing seat that hung down from the roof beams. He skilfully moved the bar of sandwiched iron and steel back and forth so that each fast blow fell on to a different part of the blade that he formed.

Jack Price, his son, was heater lad. He held the bars of metal in the fire with tongs. At last Mr Price gave his son the nod and the steeling hammer was stopped. The hammers worked in twenty minute bursts, then there was seven minutes of peace and quiet while they sorted themselves out and got ready for the next round.

Jack winked at William. "Is this one of your Maggie's little uns?"

"No," said Ben. "He's a poor dead grinder's child, and he's coming to live with me."

Ben told them the sad story and both the forgeman and his son listened with sympathy. William stared up round-eyed at the bellows that continued to puff and blow even though the hammer was stilled.

Foregemaster Price shook his head. "I can see you've taken something on, all right. I should think my missus will be glad to help out and give your nan a rest. She misses having youngsters around."

Ben thanked him politely. It seemed that help was coming from all around. Almost too much, thought Ben. After all, he was the one that had first wanted William. The Prices lived next door to the Sterndales in the small row of workmen's cottages. The melter and his family lived on the other side. They'd have the whole Works taking William on at this rate.

Ruth sneaked away from her packing work to join them.

"I could watch him for you," she said. "I could see that he's safe, if you want to get back to your work."

Ben didn't want to, but he thought that he'd better. "Thanks," he muttered. "Bring him back down to my dad if he's a nuisance. He doesn't seem to be scared of the hammer now he's seen where all the thumping's coming from."

"Right," said Jack Price. "Frightened or not, we must get this hammer going again. Are you ready to start up, Dad?"

"They're going to bang again," Ben warned William. "Do you want to see?"

The close-cropped head nodded vigorously. "Boy see bang," he whispered.

Ben went back to the melting shop, leaving William and Ruth happily watching the hammer.

When Ben got back to the cottage that evening he found Nan in good spirits, lines of clean washing already half-dry, and the food cooking steadily. The scrap of grinder's rag was lying discarded on the settle.

"Where's William?" he asked, fearing that Mrs Price had already laid claim to him.

"Out in the woods with Mort," Nan told him. "They're good chaps, I must say that. I walked up there with William when I'd put my things out to dry. They said I was to leave him. You're to fetch him back when you're ready."

"I'll go straight up," said Ben. "I'll wash later."

He hurried through the woods feeling strangely bothered. He knew that the two men were kind, but would William be scared to be left with them? Would they understand how easily he might run off and get lost?

There was no need to worry; he found William happily helping Mort to lay out sticks in a careful circle, ready to start another wood stack. The Book-Fuddler sat in his usual place with his nose in a newspaper.

"There you are," said Ben breathlessly. "Time to come home with me."

"No," said William, shaking his head. "Boy build sticks."

"Don't worry," said Mort. "We'll have finished the bottom

layer in a minute."

The Book-Fuddler looked up from his newspaper.

"Have you been reading that pamphlet I gave you?"

Ben frowned. Hadn't he had enough to do, without reading pamphlets? Anyway, each time he'd tried, the words and letters seemed to jump around and make no sense.

"Been too busy," he said.

The Book-Fuddler smiled. "If you bring it here sometime, I could help you. Reading's better when there's two to sort it out."

"Aye," said Ben. He did wish that he could read properly. "I know some of my letters, but it's hard to spell out the words."

"I'll be pleased to help," the man told him. "It gives you power, does reading and writing. Power to say what you think and write it all down . . . send it wherever you want."

Ben stared at the thin man. It was a kind offer, but something about his words made Ben think of the mysterious message that had come from Mary Ann. Write it all down and send it where you want. Wasn't that what the messenger had done?

"There's been a right to-do down at the Works today," Ben said innocently. "They say Mary Ann has been."

"Do they?" The Book-Fuddler was certainly not surprised by the news.

Ben sat down beside him determined to find out more. "Who is this Mary Ann who brings these messages?"

The Book-Fuddler smiled and waved his hands airily at the trees. "She is the beautiful Spirit of Freedom! She is the Lady of Liberty. She is all about us, though we cannot see her, standing with those who seek justice."

Ben frowned with frustration. That was not the answer he wanted. What was he supposed to make of that? Was Mary

Ann some kind of ghost? Why did this chap have to be so kind yet so annoying?

Mort looked up from his work and laughed at Ben's puzzled expression. "You'll get no sense from him, Ben! Have you not heard what happened up at Top Totley Works?"

Ben shook his head.

"Well the bosses up there took on non-Union men for saw grinding and Mary Ann paid them a few visits. First she came one night and stole the bands from the main grinding drum. That was the first warning. Then she sent a written message. The bosses took not a blind bit of notice and next thing they knew the great water wheel was smashed to pieces one night, and MARY ANN'S REVENGE daubed on the walls."

Ben thought that perhaps he was beginning to understand. "So it's Union men who do it and call themselves Mary Ann. It's not a woman at all?"

"It's better not to ask who does it," the Book-Fuddler spoke again. "That message to Dyson has come from working folk hard pressed for money and jobs. Whoever has written the message and delivered it . . . they speak for a lot of us."

Ben still suspected that the Book-Fuddler knew more than he let on. "Would they be in trouble then, if they were caught? Do they say it's Mary Ann to disguise themselves?"

"I daresay there would be trouble," the man spoke without concern. Just for a moment a frightening thought came creeping into Ben's mind. Why had his father been up so late last night? Why had he been so tired and snappy in the morning? Surely it couldn't be him doing these things? He'd always been such a quiet law-abiding man and besides – Ben heaved a sigh of relief – he couldn't even read and write. No, it couldn't be his father writing the messages.

"I'm glad to hear as your father's bent on keeping that little lad," the Book-Fuddler suddenly said, shocking him and making his heart beat fast. It was almost as though he knew Ben's thoughts.

"I think you helped," Ben told him. "It was good, that bit that you read in the alehouse."

"Don't know what you mean," said the Book-Fuddler with a smile and a wink. He turned back to his newspaper.

"Come on, William," said Ben. "You're coming home with me *now*."

CHAPTER TWELVE

The Sacred Month

THE WEEKS that followed were hot and sticky; the Scythe Works was a roasting, smelly place to live and work. Despite the rude whistles and shouts of the forgemen, the packing women stripped off their shawls and heavy linen skirts and clattered around the yard in their clogs, wearing only their shifts and stays. The water level in the dam sank, making it hard to finish the scythes, for water was needed both to turn the wheel and to grind the blades.

Though trade was bad all over, the demand for scythes and bill hooks stayed steady and the workers at Dyson's Yard thought themselves fortunate. Mr Dyson ignored his letter of warning and continued to keep the non-Union grinders working for him.

Through the hottest weather, Ben crept down to his father in the cool potshop whenever he could. "Phew! I know now why they call it the melting shop," he said.

His father looked up at him and laughed at his red face dripping with sweat, his damp hair sticking up in wild tufts.

"It looks as though it's thee that's melting, lad."

"Has tha work for me down here?" Ben asked hopefully.

"Aye. You can set about making lids for these pots that I've finished. I've to go over to the counting house to have a word with the clerk. That powdered clay in store will not last us more than three weeks."

Ben nodded, pleased to stay down there.

"Now . . . does tha knows what tha's doing?"

"Course I do," said Ben.

As soon as his father had climbed the steps, Ben dipped his hands into the bucket of water that stood in the corner of the potshop. He patted cold water over his forehead and cheeks. "Ah," he murmured. That was better. Cool at last. Then he looked about the workshop, trying to remember what it was that he'd been asked to do.

Ben walked past the neat row of finished pots that his father had been working on, tapping each one gently as he went. They looked like huge chunky vases, though they would never hold flowers. His mouth dropped open when he came to the last pot. The sides were still straight. His father had forgotten to shape the bonnet.

Ben fetched the metal shaper from the hook where his father kept it, then climbed up on a stool to reach the top of the crucible pot. He pressed the shaper firmly down as he'd seen his father do. The stool wobbled and Ben's hands shook. He lifted the shaper anxiously, but the clay didn't seem to have cracked or flopped. Now the last crucible pot looked just as good as the others, curving in smoothly to form the bonnet.

I'll be a potman yet, thought Ben, pleased with what he'd done.

As the weather settled and summer brought days of dry warmth, Nan fell into the habit of taking William into the woods to visit the charcoal burners. She would leave him there to play amongst the grass and trees and smoking stacks until Ben went up to collect him in the evening.

Ben grew to love his evening walks through the woods. However much his legs hurt with running and his shoulders ached with carrying, the rustle and dip of the trees in their summer green would soothe and revive him. He carried his pamphlet whenever he could remember and the Book-Fuddler would sit beside him and together they'd read out loud the words of the People's Charter.

" 'A vote for every man twenty-one years of age, of sound mind, and not undergoing punishment for crime.' That's a grand sounding thing," said Ben. "But it only speaks of men, it says nought of women. I'd think my nan would have something to say about that. And what about Jess? She's all for the Charter."

"I know your Jess," the man smiled. "She's as keen for the Charter as any man I know . . . perhaps even keener."

Sometimes the Book-Fuddler cleared a path of soft earth and drew out the letters of the alphabet with a stick. It was not long before Ben could mark out his own name and other words, too. Even William knew that there was a special letter for him. The Book-Fuddler drew out a great W in the soft earth.

"What is this?" the man asked.

"It's Boy," came the answer.

"W for William," they all bellowed, laughing despairingly.

"What will we do in the winter when you've gone?" Ben asked sadly.

"Look forward to the coming of spring," said Mort.

One hot Sunday afternoon Ben took William up to the charcoal burner's grave. Nan didn't really approve of running wild through the woods on Sunday, but Ben persuaded her that visiting the grave was more decent. The two boys stood there all scrubbed and neat in their best clothes and Ben told William the story of poor George.

William listened in silence, his eyes wide with interest. "Poor George," he said, and started to scrabble about in the soft earth beside the stone.

"What are you doing?" Ben asked puzzled. "You mustn't get your jacket dirty today. Nan will go mad at us."

William stared up at him full of determination. "Willum making dinner for George," he said.

Ben could not help but smile. He settled himself down beneath the young saplings and slept in the dappled sun, while William played contentedly, carrying on a one-sided conversation with George.

At the beginning of August, news came of strikes in Lancashire. The cotton spinners and weavers who worked in the new factories were asking for better wages. It was not long before the bobbin weavers, the masons and the nailors had joined them.

August had always been known as the sacred month. The month of heat, the month of wakes and fairs, the month of struggle and strife. Placards and notices demanding support for the strikers appeared all over Sheffield Town. Ben came back from Widow Blackitt's breathless with the news.

"You should see them," he told the melting team. "Big posters! They're plastered all over the walls of the Scythe Works. They're even on the gate posts."

"What do they say?" the men asked him.

"Strike for the Charter!"

The men looked at each other uncomfortably. "They weren't there this morning."

"No . . . there was nought!"

"Say nowt," growled old Joe. "They'll be down fast enough when Dyson sees them."

Sure enough the office clerk spent the whole afternoon carefully taking them down, but they were replaced the following morning.

The second week in August Jack Carter arrived while the workers were sitting out in the sunny yard, enjoying their dinners of bread and cheese.

"What's the news today, Jack," cried Elsie cheerfully.

"Tha'll not look so merry when I tell thee what's coming," said Jack.

"Whatever can tha mean?"

The workers clustered around him in consternation.

"Gangs of 'em, hundreds of 'em . . . seen 'em myself, straggling down the roads from Halifax and Huddersfield. I've never seen such a desperate tattered lot. They're crazed with hunger and armed with pitchforks and pikes and they sing as they go . . . oh God, how they sing! They've gangs of women with them, marching in front carrying banners."

"Heaven help us," cried Elsie. "Where are they going?"

"They're marching from town to town and city to city, spreading the word. Wherever there's workers and factories."

"What is it they want?" asked Jess, frowning with the effort to understand.

"They've declared their strike to be for the Charter now. They want you to join them. Knock yer bands off! Stop your wheels and hammers! Pull out your boiler plugs! We should bring our working towns to a standstill, they say. All labour must cease, until we have our Charter Law."

"Whatever shall we do?" Elsie was frantic. "Whatever are all those women after? They'll not get any vote!"

"Nay," said Jess. "It's their bairns that they're thinking of. They want things to be better for all of us! We should join 'em, I say," Jess was red in the face with excitement. "Haven't we had enough of Parliament turning our petitions down?"

"Aye," said Frank in his slow, thoughtful way. "But a strike in Sheffield's no easy thing. Half the workers are laid off to start with; we'd soon starve and the masters'd laugh!"

"The Sheffield Chartists are having a meeting," Jack told them. "A grand meeting in Paradise Square on Saturday. They shall decide whether Sheffield should join the strikers or not. You should come to it and have your say."

Ben's father went along to the meeting with old Joe and Jess. Ruth spent a blessed day of freedom in the woods with Ben and William, but she did not seem her usual cheerful bossy self. Even William could hardly get a smile from her. Whenever Ben spoke of the Chartists' meeting, she frowned and ignored him. They all met up in the evening in Nan's kitchen for a sup of ale.

"Well, I don't think there'll be strikes in Sheffield," Ben's father told them. "Though the arguments have been fierce."

"Well I for one am glad of that," said Nan.

"And me," said Ruth.

"Aye well," Jess agreed reluctantly. "We have to face it, Sheffield is a very different place from Manchester. Those poor mill workers are treated terribly, but if *they* strike, they can bring those mills to a standstill and ruin their bosses. Here in Sheffield, it's always been a struggle to keep working through the summer months. Our bosses'll be glad of any excuse to lay us off."

"Aye," said Frank. "I think Mr Harney understands it now. Who is there left to strike in Sheffield, what with the slump in trade and the water shortage?"

"I've been reading what the People's Charter says," said Ben.

"Good lad," Jess kissed his cheek, making him blush.

"I know you're for the Charter, Jess, but I'm thinking you should be wanting votes for women? Don't you want your own vote, too?"

Jess shook her head sadly. "Of course I do, no doubt of that! Maybe votes for our men will bring it nearer to us. The day will come," she said. "The day will come for women, too."

There was a thoughtful silence while they looked on smiling at William who played a pat-a-cake game with Ruth.

"I can't believe that's the same bairn you brought back from the Workhouse," said Jess.

"Aye," Nan agreed with pride. "Our Maggie was saying the same when they came visiting last week. She couldn't believe how well he looks, and how he hugged and kissed her. D'you know, he calls me Nan and there's no sign left of that dreadful cough he used to have."

"Good boy, William!" said Ruth, tickling him.

"Yes," said Ben, with almost fatherly pride. "And his special grinder's rag is kept upstairs now. He only needs it at night."

All through the middle of the month there were lively meetings in Paradise Square. Mr Harney went back and forth over the Pennines to consult with the Lancashire Chartists. News came of a great clash between the strikers and soldiers on the Halifax to Elland road, two Chartists killed and others wounded. Strikers had been arrested and taken to Wakefield gaol. At Leeds and Cleckheaton, support for the strike seemed to be fading. Troops and special constables were called in to prevent the strikers entering the towns.

It was not long before another huge meeting was called for by the Sheffield Chartists. A meeting which went on from Friday evening, through Saturday and Sunday, as more and more people flooded into the Paradise Square and joined fiercely in the arguments. On Monday the square was packed to bursting. Ben walked into Sheffield to join them with his father and Jess.

"Strike for the Charter! Strike for the vote!" Jess bellowed excitedly, waving her fist at the men who stood on the raised steps.

Both Ben and his father watched her with smiling admiration, but at the end of the day it was agreed that Sheffield could not manage a strike at that time of year. They'd show their support by holding a great parade through the streets. Sheffield was for the Charter, through and through, but all it had to offer was workless artisans with starving families, desperately trying to struggle through a slump and a hot dry summer.

Maggie and John turned up with all their children. They were having a hard time of it as John was short of work.

"Come up to the Cutler's Arms," said Frank. "At least I can buy you ale and a little food for my grandchildren. I know that your nan will be coming down too next Monday with puddings and ham."

So they all walked together, up to the Cutler's Arms. Dan the Book-Fuddler was there deep in conversation with the Thorpe brothers.

"Ah," said Jess. "I've something to say to those fellows," and she went marching over to talk to them.

Ben thought that his father looked anxious when he saw them all with their heads together.

"There's trouble brewing there, I'll swear," John said. "Maybe trouble for you up at Dyson's Yard. There'll be more visits from Mary Ann, I daresay. There'll be grinding bands pulled off next!"

Frank shook his head. "Not in our grinding hull," he said. "But I fear tha speaks the truth when tha speaks of trouble. I hear that the Thorpes are short of work and short of water.

Strong Union chaps like them, they'll find it hard to stand by and see Dyson with his cheap labour."

"Aye, there's bitter talk of Dyson," said John shaking his head. "When so many grinders are struggling, they're sore to see non-Union men working up at Abbeydale. You'll have to look out for Mary Ann."

Frank sighed. "I always look out for Mary Ann."

"Why is it always the grinders that are so fierce and fearless?" said Ben.

Suddenly Maggie's eyes filled up with tears and Frank seemed lost for words.

It was John himself answered him, smiling and speaking gently. "When work brings early death with it, why what else has tha to fear?"

CHAPTER THIRTEEN

The Puller-Out

A S THE SACRED MONTH drew to a close, the weather cooled. Heavy rain brought mud and mess and better supplies of water. Work picked up a little and those who'd struggled through the summer saw some small signs of hope ahead. News of the marching strikers became sparse. It seemed they'd come as far south as Barnsley, but no further. Many of them had been arrested and gaoled, and some sent off to Australia.

One chilly morning late in October, Ben was enjoying the steady build-up of heat in the melting shop. For an hour or so it was pleasant and comfortable while he and Cokey lowered the crucibles carefully into the furnace holes. They packed coke around the pots and chatted while the heat rose.

"How's that wild little bairn of yours?"

"He's champion," said Ben. "He wears my nan out though. He wears me out an' all."

When the melter and old Joe arrived, they inspected the crucible pots heating slowly in the holes.

"Aye," said the melter. "They're ready to be filled."

The puller-out fetched the charge pans down from the weighing shop, and the melter lowered the carefully weighed pieces of blister steel gently down into the heating pots through a great iron funnel.

By mid-morning any pleasure in the warmth was gone. Sweat poured from all the workers. The journeys up and down the cellar stairs became more wearisome, but the hearths must be kept clear of ash so that the draught of searing hot air would sweep up around the furnace holes. Ben went back and forth, his head spinning. He swore and grumbled as he grew hotter and hotter; his face and hair coated with ash.

"Ale!" the puller-out bellowed. Ben jumped to his feet. A quick run to Widow Blackitt's would be a blessed relief.

He came back feeling better for the small sup of ale that Widow Blackitt had offered him, but the men were restless and snappy, waiting for their drink.

"Drat the lad!" the puller-out clouted him. "Here's us stood about waiting for ale and this pot ready to be pulled."

Ben hurriedly poured their drinks, then turned back to the water trough, ready to wet the puller-out's rags for him.

"Come on then, Nipper," he snarled. "We'll not wait till Sunday!"

Ben slopped water all over Joe's sacking-bound legs and feet. The puller-out shook himself like a dog and took up his straight tongs. The melter lifted up the furnace cover and looked up at the puller-out.

"What's tha think?"

"Aye. Looks killed to me."

He gripped the side of the crucible with his tongs and began to haul it up and out of the furnace hole. Ben picked up the half empty jug of ale and backed mouse-like into the corner of the teeming bay. The pot came out glowing golden white and sparking a little. The melter picked up his curved tongs ready to pour the steel. As the puller-out moved the crucible swiftly towards the teeming bay, the melter suddenly cried out, "Watch its bonnet!"

"Damn!" the puller-out growled. "It's going! Bonnet's off! Bonnet's o . . . ff!"

It was a desperate cry. A terrible cry. There was scuffling and thuds as men ran fast for the doorway, but Ben's legs seemed to have turned to stone. A dreadful moment of silence was broken by the sudden flare and spitting from the cracked top of the glowing crucible. A trickle of molten steel spilled out and snaked its way across the floor of the teeming bay. Ben gasped but still he could not seem to move. The white hot metal crackled and spat, cutting off his pathway to the door. The ale jug slipped from his hands, splashing on to the oozing white hot metal, sprinkling it with drops that burst into flames and hissed with steam.

Ben took breath at last.

"Da . . . ad!" he cried, a wild and hopeless scream.

He saw his father's frantic face at the top of the pot shop stairs; then the melter's broad shoulders blocked the doorway.

"Da . . . ad!" Now that he had begun to scream he couldn't stop.

The puller-out appeared in the doorway alongside the melter. "Shut tha noise!" he bellowed. Ben gasped and stopped. Didn't he always obey old Joe?

Calmly the puller-out took the curved tongs from the melter's hands, and set them diving across the flames like a black snapping mouth. He clamped them tightly around Ben's waist and braced himself. He heaved the lad high into the air above the exploding steel. One minute Ben went flying up towards the roof, the next he came swooping back down on top of the melter and the puller-out, still crammed together in the doorway. The shock of Ben's weight sent them toppling backwards down the stone steps.

A great jumble of bodies went bumping painfully out into Dyson's Yard. The packing women started shrieking till the men from the blacking shop came rushing out to see what was going on.

"What the heck is tha doing?" yelled Elsie. "What the heck? Tha's too big to play at roly poly!"

Ben could not stop shaking. His father came running down the steps behind him. He picked him up and wrapped his arms around him. All work stopped, while everyone argued and fussed. At last John Dyson came out of his office.

"Is the lad all right?" he asked.

Ben got up, though his knees were still shaking. "Aye. I'm fine, sir." And though his head and elbows were battered from the fall down the steps, he did seem to be unharmed.

CASTING CRUCIBLE STEEL.
1. Casting. 2. Watching the Furnace. 3. Funnel for Filling Pots in the Furnace.

Suddenly a quietness fell on all the workers. Dyson strode over to where Ben's father was still crouched at the bottom of the steps. Everyone held their breath, but the man spoke without anger.

"Not like you, Frank," he said. "Not like you to turn out a bad pot."

Frank Sterndale's face was white. He shook his head, but said nothing.

"Well . . . no harm done it seems. Back to work! All of you back to work!"

Ben watched his father worriedly. While most of the other men got back to work, his father sat on at the bottom of the steps. As though they'd both had the same thought at once, Jess and Ben swooped down on him.

"Come on now, Frank," Jess soothed, taking his hands and pulling him to his feet. "Ben is fine and there's no real hurt done."

"There's nowt to worry about," Ben told him, swallowing hard.

His father answered him sharply. "If a bonnet's off, it's a bad pot. They'll not trust me the same. I've never made a bad pot in my life."

A small but uncomfortable doubt entered Ben's head at that moment, but before he could speak, his father snatched his arm and pulled him over the yard to where the puller-out sat rubbing his knee. "There's something must be said," he muttered. He bent down and took hold of Joe's scarred hand in both of his smooth clay-dusted ones.

"I thank thee," he said. "I thank thee from the bottom of my heart. Tha's saved our Ben."

The puller-out shrugged his shoulders and grinned toothlessly. "Just doing my job," he said. "What else should a puller-out do?" He cleared his throat and spat on Ben's clogs.

Nan was in a right taking when she heard about the accident. Ben tried to reassure her that nothing dreadful had come of it.

"It's not what happened," she snapped. "It's what might have happened. I've known men sacked for turning out one bad pot. The melting team have got to have faith in their potman or they just can't work."

Ben listened to it all and felt deeply miserable. There was one pot on those shelves that had not been made by his father, or at least it had not been finished by him. Ben remembered the pride he'd felt when he pressed the shaper down and finished the pot himself. He also remembered his surprise when he'd felt the clay give. Had that been all wrong? Was that the bad pot? Would he be sacked if he told them what he'd done?

All through the week that followed, the yard was full of whispers. The atmosphere was tense; even the packing women seemed to have lost their usual cheerful rudeness.

Ben could not sleep at nights for worrying about that pot. He was short-tempered with William, though he saw enough to know that Ruth was as miserable and tired as himself.

"Will you come up through the woods with me tonight?" he asked her, hoping somehow to cheer her.

"Aye," she said, with a faint smile. "Is the bairn still stopping with the charcoal burners?"

"Yes," Ben told her. "But not for long. They're packing up for winter; just finishing off the stacks and they'll be going. William'll have to stay at home soon."

The light was failing as they walked through the woods to the charcoal burner's clearing. The trees seemed to echo their sadness; leaves floated down from the branches to rest in scattered heaps in the mud.

Even the Book-Fuddler was not his usual patient self. He shouted at Ben when he started to help lift the freshly cooled charcoal from a stack and put it into one of the piles.

"Leave be!" he told him. "That's the wrong lot you're putting there."

Ben shrugged his shoulders, offended. "Only trying to help," he said. "Thought charcoal was all the same."

"What?" the Book-Fuddler shouted. Then seeing Ben's misery he sighed and smiled. He patted Ben's shoulder and spoke in his usual friendly way. "Nay, lad, charcoal's different for different purposes. This lot's the finest stuff, all smoked from alder trees. Mort's boy is coming with a cart to fetch it and take it up to Wharncliffe where he works."

"What's it for?" Ben asked, faintly interested.

The Book-Fuddler winked. "Making gunpowder," he said.

All three of them were quiet as they walked back through the woods. Ben knew that Ruth was troubled and he tried a bit of clumsy clowning to cheer her, sticking leaves in William's now thick hair and calling them ears. But Ruth only smiled weakly and Ben gave up. He'd too much on his own mind to worry about her.

CHAPTER FOURTEEN

November the Fifth

EN SPENT more sleepless nights and found his patience with William wearing thin. The weather had turned very wintery and once again Sheffield town was full of fear and strife. The thought of another hard winter coming so early was terrible to the poorest folk. Out at Dyson's Yard work continued steadily, though there was much resentment of the grinders who still worked there though they paid no Union dues.

The workers built a bonfire on November the fifth and there was singing and dancing in the yard. The grinders' apprentices made a straw-stuffed guy that was set upon the fire to the sounds of wild clapping and cheering. There were whispers that with its tall hat and sacking cloak painted in the blacking shop, it bore a noticeable resemblance to Mr Dyson. However, the owner himself did not appear to notice it. He sent ale out to the workers from his kitchen and fresh baked oatcakes which were eaten with relish.

Jack Price took up his squeeze box and played a cheerful tune. Elsie and Jess strode out in their clogs to perform the special scythe-makers' steps.

"Come on . . . all the gang!" they shouted.

Some of the packing women followed them eagerly, others had to be pushed and teased, but at last they all held up their skirts and jigged up and down, clattering their clogs on the stone flags. The intricate steps that they performed echoed the everyday working sounds of the Scythe Works.

"In an' out the fire," yelled Elsie.

"Now swing the blade," Jess told them.

At once they swung their legs out to the side, just as the forgemaster swung the scythe blade back and forth beneath the hammer.

Nan brought her rocking chair outside and wrapping a warm blanket about them both, she took William up on her knee. Mrs Price brought William sticky toffee made from black treacle and butter. He and Nan rocked gently back and forth together in time with the clattering of the clogs.

William's eyes opened wide as Jess beat out the fast rhythm of the steeling hammer. She held her body stiff and straight, but her legs and feet moved at such a pace that you couldn't see each stamp and tap. Elsie clumped up and down beside her, echoing the slower rhythm of the plating hammer while the workers clapped along with them.

Ben could not join in the celebration. He watched them from the shadowy corner beside the still waterwheel. All day he'd felt sick in his stomach, believing that the tension in the Works came from mistrust of his father. How could any of them trust a potman whose crucible pots collapsed? Even Jess who'd always been their special friend had spoken angrily that day. She'd got up from the stone steps where she'd been sitting eating her bread and cheese with them, and marched away red faced to join Elsie, crying out, "I'd never have thought it of thee, Frank Sterndale!"

Ben looked over to where his father sat with Forgemaster Price; though he nodded his head in time to the music his face was drawn and anxious.

They'll never trust him again, thought Ben. Maybe he'll never trust himself . . . and it's all my fault.

Ben was so taken up with his own misery that at first he

didn't notice when someone came up beside him in the darkness.

"Now then, lad," the growling voice of the puller-out spoke in his ear. "I think thou owes me summat!"

Ben shuddered. Weren't things bad enough without this?

"Thou owes me! Isn't that so?"

"Aye," said Ben. "I owe thee."

"Right," said Joe. "Tha can pay me, then. Tha knows that lanky charcoal burner?"

"Aye," said Ben, warily. "The one they call the Book-Fuddler?"

"That's the one! Go find him, lad, and tell him this: Mary Ann will be visiting tonight!"

Ben caught his breath and his legs went all wobbly. "Now?"

"Aye," said Joe calmly. "Right now!"

Ben walked quietly back to the cottages, past Nan and William and his own doorway. He said nothing to them though his whole body was trembling. Out he went through Dyson's gate, into the dark woods.

Although he'd lived beside them all his life, he'd never been out so late at night amongst the trees. The woods were full of falling leaves and rustling shadows. The darkness was frightening, but Ben was so full of guilt and worry that the vague indefinable fear brought by faint sounds and shadows was almost a relief. He marched onwards, ignoring the crackling of twigs under his feet, following his usual path almost without thinking.

He'd walked far from the cart track before he stopped. He looked around him with satisfaction. A great sigh welled up in his throat and seeped out into the silence; then he jumped at the faint snap of wood behind him.

Just a rabbit, he told himself, but as he turned he caught a movement of dark shadow that slipped from one solid tree trunk to the next.

"Who is it?" His voice croaked.

"'S me . . . Ruth. Seen you go."

His relief quickly turned to irritation. "What you doing? Can't you leave me alone?"

There was no reply. Why wasn't she dancing and prancing about with the others. Hadn't he seen her clattering her clogs and jigging about? He huffed and puffed with impatience, but he took a few steps towards her and caught the faint sound of a sob.

"What's wrong?" he managed to ask, more kindly.

"Can't say! Can't tell!" she whispered, her shoulders shaking.

Ben put out his hand and touched her arm. Such a dark forlorn shape she made, shivering and crying quietly amongst the trees, that Ben could not help but forget his own worries for the moment.

"You're freezing. Better get you warm. Come on," he said, thinking fast. "The charcoal burners are closer than home and I've got to see them. They'll have a fire going."

Ruth clutched on to his sleeve and he led her confidently through the darkness.

Mort was resting with his back against the cone-shaped turf-covered hut. They approached so quietly, not speaking to each other, that he looked up with a shock to see their anxious young faces gleaming pale and golden in the light that his fire threw.

"What the devil?"

"We're cold, Mort," Ben told him. "Ruth can't stop shivering and everything's going wrong."

It was not long before they were both sitting in front of a glowing fire that threw out a good heat. Mort wrapped a thick woollen coat round Ruth's shoulders and warmed up a bowl of rabbit stew for her.

"Oh I couldn't," she shook her head, but Mort insisted and fed her a few spoonfuls. At the sound of voices, the Book-Fuddler crawled from the turf-stacked hut. He took in the situation at a glance and sat down beside them at the fire without a word.

"Ruth followed me into the woods," Ben explained. "She's terrible upset."

Ruth continued to stare into the glowing fire as though he'd never spoken.

"And I've a message for thee. It comes from old Joe, the puller-out."

Ben bent close and whispered his message into Dan's ear. Ruth looked up at them and gave a cry of utter dismay.

"What is it?" Ben asked.

"I heard," she whispered. "I heard what you said . . . that name!"

Ben turned from Ruth to Dan, shaken and puzzled.

The Book-Fuddler spoke gently. "I can guess what ails thee little lass," he said. "You are fearful for Mary Ann!"

Ruth's chin trembled as though she wanted to cry again, but at last she nodded her head.

"You needn't fear to speak of it here," he said. "We are all your friends and the woods surround us with silence. I gather she'll be visiting tonight."

"She?" said Ben. He almost wanted to laugh. The puller-out was the funniest kind of woman that he could think of. "But Mary Ann's no woman," he said.

Ruth stared at him, silent and white-faced in the firelight.

Ben could not understand. Why was she looking like that? It was then that the worrying thought came to him. What if after all Mary Ann was a woman? Why shouldn't it be a woman, if there was a woman daft and brave enough to do it? Then suddenly he knew. He knew it all.

"It's Jess," he said. "It's Jess that delivers the message from Mary Ann."

Ruth's eyes filled up with tears again.

Ben sighed, understanding much better now. He should have known it all along. Reckless Jess, with her anger and her passionate devotion to the grinders and their Union. She could write too, couldn't she? Wasn't it Jess that taught all the melting team to write their names for the petition?

"What is it that she does?" he asked.

"She writes a message out on paper. Then she delivers it to Mr Dyson's office in the middle of the night," Ruth told him.

"But what is so terrible about that?"

Ruth shrugged her shoulders. "It's what it says, I suppose. UNION MEN ONLY OR THE DEVIL SHALL COME FOR THEE. Then she signs it MARY ANN."

"Oh!" Ben was a little shaken by the strength of the words. "Would that cause such trouble?"

"Oh aye," said Mort. "Threatening letter, the constables would call it."

The Book-Fuddler nodded. " 'Conspiracy to incite', maybe 'seditious conspiracy'. But try not to be so fearful little lass," he told her. "When your mother takes that message, she speaks for many of us. She's a brave lass, but she's clever too. She'll not get caught, I'm sure of it."

Ben turned to Ruth. He wrapped his arm around her shoulders and hugged her. "She's a brave one is your mam," he said.

"I wish she weren't," whispered Ruth. "If she were caught they'd maybe send her off to prison or even to Australy like they did the strikers. I wish she'd take notice of your dad. He's done his best to persuade her out of it, but she'll not listen."

Ben's mouth dropped open. "Is that it? Is that why she was angry with him?"

"Aye," said Ruth. "What else?"

Ben smiled foolishly. "Nowt," he said. He'd been so caught up with his own guilt and fears that he'd not seen the bigger dangers about him.

Ben shook his head, thinking of the bonfire and the singing. "How can she? How can she sing and dance like that? Knowing what she's to do!"

The Book-Fuddler smiled. "That's the cleverness of her," he said. "Who would suspect? Who would be looking for Mary Ann on such a night as this."

CHAPTER FIFTEEN

Time to be Brave

THE BOOK-FUDDLER walked back through the woods with them, lighting their way with a lantern. Dyson's Works were quiet, the remains of the bonfire glowing faintly in the dark.

"I shall walk you back to your cottage," the Book-Fuddler said to Ruth.

"Aye," she said. "I'd be glad of it."

"Shall I wait with you till Jess returns?"

Ruth nodded gratefully.

"I'd best get back to Nan," Ben said, then hesitantly he turned to Ruth, his voice grown husky and solemn. "Don't fear that I know about Mary Ann. I'd rather die than give her away."

Ruth snatched up his hands. "I know it," she said and kissed him on the cheek.

As Ben left them, he caught the faint sound of a happy giggle. He smiled, for it was the first joyful sound that Ruth had made for weeks. He stumbled up the pathway past Nan's cabbages to the back door, glad that the night hid his blushes.

Ben's father was still up and dressed.

"Wherever has tha been, lad?" he cried. "Your nan's that bothered!"

"Sorry. Been out in the woods with Ruth and the charcoal burners."

"Ruth? Is she all right?"

"Aye . . . she's fine. Lanky Dan has taken her home."

"Ah." He looked relieved and opened his mouth as though he'd like to say more, but then changed his mind. "Well, we've had trouble getting that young un off to bed! All he wanted was you. Eh dear, you should have heard him. 'Where's Ben? Want Ben?'"

Ben couldn't help but smile at that, but he saw that his father looked grey with weariness. He smelt of the bonfire and ale. For some strange reason Ben felt somehow better and braver. Braver than he'd felt for days; ever since the accident really. He wanted to tell his father about the cracked crucible there and then, but he could see that there were other things on Frank's mind. Time enough in the morning for speaking up.

His father came over and ruffled his hair. "You go on up and see the little lad. Your nan's just got him settled and off to bed herself."

"Aren't you coming up?"

"In a minute . . . just a bit restless."

Ben understood this time.

"Dad?" he said. "I know what you're up to. You're watching for Mary Ann. Ruth has told me. Don't fear that I'd ever say ought about it."

Frank sighed. "Ey son! She does bother me, does Jess. I dread to think what would happen to her were she found out."

Ben nodded. "It's worrying Ruth frantic, too. Why is she doing it? Isn't it Union men that usually do the job of Mary Ann."

"Aye, by rights it is! And they don't usually just send written messages. You know what happened at Top Totley?"

Ben nodded.

"She's partly doing it because of her poor husband. But it's more than that. She's trying to act as go-between. Doing her best to warn Dyson and stop him in his tracks. But if he will not listen this time and take on Union men, I fear there'll be no holding them back. There's folk very angry with Dyson." Frank put his arm around Ben's shoulders. "Now you get on off to bed, son, and try not to worry about it all. I must just see for myself that Mary Ann gets safely home tonight."

Ben was too sleepy to argue any more.

The following morning Ben woke early. He vaguely remembered hearing his father's footsteps coming upstairs in the middle of the night. Even though he'd been half asleep, a sense of relief had come to him; Mary Ann must have been and gone without trouble.

William slept beside him, his cheeks smudged with soot from the bonfire and his mouth smeared at the corners with melted black treacle toffee. Ben smiled. Nan must have been very tired after the bonfire for William had clearly escaped the dreaded wash.

When Ben had climbed the ladder last night, he'd found the little boy puffy eyed and tear stained, lying awake in bed, tightly clutching his rag.

"Ben come back?" he whispered happily.

"Yes, Ben's come back," he'd told him, snappy with exhaustion. "Now shift up, I'm tired out."

William had given him a sticky kiss and snuggled up close to him. He'd fallen asleep almost immediately.

Ben had lain there beside him, his arms wrapped round the small body. "Oh yes, Ben's back," he said with determination. "And he's got something to put right."

It was mid morning when the clerk walked over to the grinding hull and asked the two non-Union grinders to step over to the office and see Mr Dyson. The news shot around the Works as fast as a running rabbit. The other grinders stopped their work and spoke in quiet hopeful voices. The yard was full of whispering and watching eyes, only Jess seemed unbothered, carrying on cheerfully with her straw plaiting.

At last the door of the office opened and the two men walked out. They crossed the yard, back to the grinding hull, their faces blank. Would they pick up their coats and go? Moments passed, a minute went by. Then the droning whine of their grinding wheels started up. Elsie strode over the yard to the grinding hull.

"They're set on again!" she cried, her pink cheeks quivering.

A deep shocked groan seemed to come from all around. Then a bleak blank quietness. Gradually the workers turned back to their tasks, heads shaking, voices low.

Ben was up on the top step of the crucible workshop, lifting the heavy wooden yoke on to his shoulders, ready for his walk to Widow Blackitt's when he saw something that made his heart thump. Jess was leaning forward over one of the boxes, half packed with newly blackened scythes. Her shoulders shook and her face was hidden. At first he thought that she was laughing, but Ruth ran white-faced to her mother's side. Then he understood. She was not laughing, not laughing at all; she was crying. Great racking sobs shook her whole body and made the other women stare with fear.

"She'll give herself away," he whispered. Ben dropped his yoke and ran to fetch his father.

Frank Sterndale left his pots immediately. He leapt down the steps into the yard, pushing aside the fussing packers.

"Is it the sickness?" they murmured.

"She's taking a fit!"

"Is she mad?"

Frank bent over Jess, putting his hand on to her forehead.

"That's it!" she sobbed wildly. "Can't hold them back! Can't hold them back any more. Tried so hard . . . tried to warn him!"

"Fever," Ben's father said firmly. "Sick with the fever. She must rest, Elsie can take charge."

"Cholera!"

"Typhus!"

The packing women stood quickly back as Ben's father grabbed Jess around the waist and marched her over to his own cottage, Ben and Ruth following in his wake.

Nan was thrown into a tizzy. "Sage tea! That's what's needed. Put the kettle on, Ben!"

She set about rubbing Jess's hands. William sat quiet and still, watching them all with puzzled eyes. Frank quickly made Jess comfortable on the settle by the fire. He fetched the rug from his own bed to wrap her in.

Ruth was trembling and fearful. "The fever . . . oh, what shall we do?"

"Don't fret Ruth," Ben's father answered quickly. "I doubt it's really the fever. More like shock. Shock and despair! Look how she's worked to get rid of those grinders in a peaceable way! She's done what she could, risked all! It's out of our hands now. Dyson must take what comes."

Jess sipped Nan's strong sage tea, and was soon calmed by it.

"I must get back to Elsie."

"Oh no you don't, I've told them you're sick, and sick you shall be!" Frank insisted. "Ruth, take your mother home and keep her there for the rest of the day!"

Jess opened her mouth to disagree, but shut it at the sight of Frank's determined face.

"For your own safety, Jess," he said more gently. "Tha knows tha cannot keep quiet when things are going wrong! Leave be and let Ruth take thee home."

Ben followed his father over the yard back to the workshop. "She's a brave un," he said.

"Aye. Too brave for her own good," Frank answered him quite sharply.

"Yes," said Ben. And the thought came to him that maybe what he was planning to say would be best kept quiet for his own good. But then he shrugged his shoulders. Nay, he thought. Time for me to be brave too.

Ben picked his moment carefully. He served all the men with ale and made sure that the workshop was quiet, the crucible pots heating steadily but not yet ready for pouring.

He went down to his father and told him that the melter wanted a word with him. His father looked surprised, but he left the pot he was finishing and went straight upstairs to the melting shop.

"What is it?" he asked the melter.

"What's what, Frank?" the melter was puzzled.

Ben swallowed hard. "I've summat to tell," he said, his voice high-pitched and shaky.

The men stared at him. The cellar lad? The young nipper? He'd no business telling anybody anything! His job was to do as he was told and say nowt!

"What the blazes?" the puller-out growled.

"It was me," said Ben. "It was me as finished that pot, not my dad."

"Ey?" the melter was still mystified.

"Ben?" his father frowned at him.

"It was me that finished that pot – the one that spilled. I'm sorry, Dad. I pressed the shaper down, when you'd gone out. I must have done it wrong. My father . . ." his voice had grown wonderfully loud and shrill. "My father's never made a bad pot in his life."

There was tense silence.

"Ey Ben!" his father said, sighing.

A deep growling grunt came from old Joe, followed by another and another. Ben looked over at him with fear, but then he saw that the man was bursting with wanting to laugh out loud. All at once the puller-out stepped across the teeming bay and slapped Ben on the back. "Well, lad, if tha's such a rotten potman . . . why then, I say we'd better have thee on the melting team!"

Suddenly it seemed that all the men were laughing, great roaring laughs; thumping each other with wild ridiculous joy. They clutched their stomachs, eyes watering.

"Ey Ben," said his father, chuckling and wiping his eyes. "Tha's a grand lad."

"Am I not sacked?" he asked.

"Get back to work, all of thee," the melter shook his head. "And thee especially, cellar lad!"

CHAPTER SIXTEEN

The Darkest Night

J ESS AND RUTH were both back at work the following
morning, swearing that the sickness was naught but a chill
caught on bonfire night. Jess was her usual chirpy self,
resigned it seemed to whatever might come. She sat on the steps
at noon, eating her bread and cheese with Ben and his father.

"Tha's done tha best girl," Frank Sterndale told her,
speaking low. "Tha's done more than anyone could ask."

Jess shrugged her shoulders. "They've had their warning,"
she said. "I can't do more."

"What will come now?" said Ben nervously.

"I don't know. Don't want to know!" said Jess. "I've
promised Ruth my part is played. There'll be no more visits
from this Mary Ann."

It was a day of bright sunshine and Nan wandered across
the yard with William in tow. Ruth swooped down on him and
scooped him up in her arms, making him giggle and pull at her
hair.

"Just look at that bairn," Jess cried. "He's bonny and good
and happy."

Nan smiled broadly and sat down with them, groaning a bit
as her knees creaked. "He's a smashing little chap," she
agreed, "though you must thank Ben for that. I'd never have
taken him on by myself. The lad's been as patient with him as
if he were his own brother."

"Eeh Ben . . . you've made a grand job of looking after him,"
said Jess.

That night when Ben got back from work, he found Nan bouncing William on her knee by the fire and singing in her croaky old voice:

"This is the way the farmers ride,
Trot, trot, trot.
This is the way the postboys ride,
A-gallop, a-gallop, a-gallop.
And this is the way that William rides,
Hobble-di-gee, hobble-di-gee,
And . . . down in to a ditch!"

Down went William as Nan lowered him backwards on to the thick rag rug.

"More! More!" William yelled with delight, scrambling to his feet.

"Oh lor'," said Nan, so breathless that she could hardly speak.

"More! More!" cried William.

Ben picked him up. "Hush up, you brat," he told him. "Ride on my knee. You've worn our nan out!"

So Nan got up, and set about making their supper, while Ben bounced William up and down in all his dirt and dusty work clothes. "You should have taken him out in the woods," he said.

"Now that reminds me," said Nan, fishing in her pocket. "The tall one, Dan. He's been here and he left this letter. He was quite bothered about it, though he's such a quiet chap. 'Ben must read it! Must read it straight away!' he said."

Ben reached out for the note, quite puzzled.

Nan went on talking while he smoothed out the worn scrap of paper. "They'll not be there much longer," she said. "He and Mort are busy packing up and sorting out. The charcoal burning is over till the spring."

Ben suddenly stopped rocking so that William cried out at him.

"What's wrong?" said Nan.

"This letter," said Ben frowning at the carefully inked words. "BE . . . WARE, it says. BEWARE THE GRINDING HULL!"

"What?" said Nan. "Let me see? Are you sure?" Nan screwed up her eyes, trying to make sense of the letters. "I don't know! What can he mean? He's such a strange fellow."

"I'd best tell Dad," said Ben, getting up.

"Not before you've washed," said Nan.

Ben came back chilly and dripping, looking for a cloth to dry himself. Nan was sitting in her chair again with William on her knee.

"Where've you put the cloth, Nan?" he asked.

There was no reply.

William patted Nan's cheek. "Gallop a-gallop?" he cried hopefully, trying to bounce up and down.

Ben went round to them, spraying droplets of water on to the floor. "Leave her be," he said. "She's fallen asleep. Tha's worn her out."

He picked William up, even though his hands were still wet. But as he lifted the child, Nan slumped forward.

"Nan!" Ben cried, dumping William roughly on the floor. "Nan . . . what's wrong?"

He shook her shoulders, but Nan did not speak or open her eyes.

"What have you done to her?" he rounded fiercely on William. "What have you done, bad, bad boy? What have you done to my nan?"

William whimpered and backed towards the stairs, his face white and shocked.

"Go away! Get away from her!" Ben cried, then he turned and ran out of the front door. He was halfway across the yard when he saw his father coming home from work.

"Come quick," he shouted. "There's summat up with Nan!"

Frank bent over his mother, his face white with shock and sorrow. He shook his head gently. "It's no good, son. I fear she's gone and there's naught will bring her back."

"Gone?" said Ben unbelieving. "Died? She can't have. She can't! She was here . . . she was singing. William was riding on her knee."

Ben's father looked blankly about the room, rubbing his head. "Where is the bairn?" he asked.

There was no sign of William. The back door stood open just as Ben had left it when he returned from his wash.

"I don't know!" Ben cried. "I don't care! It's my Nan I want!"

Frank sighed, his eyes filled with tears. "Ey Mother," he said. "Why do you have to go and do this to us?" He dropped a kiss on to her pale forehead.

Ben stared at them. He could not understand; could not believe the words his father spoke. He watched trembling as Frank picked up his mother in his arms and tenderly carried her up the staircase.

At last Ben managed to make himself follow. "What shall I do?" he asked, hopelessly.

"Go fetch Mrs Price."

Mrs Price bustled round all flustered and kind. She brewed them tea and brought them food that they couldn't eat. She went upstairs and wept quietly as she set about washing Nan's poor worn out body.

Through the shock and blankness, a small seed of anxiety

began to grow in Ben's head. His anger with William faded and he went to look in the loft, but the child was not there. He ripped the rug off the bed and stripped away the rough linen mattress cover.

"Where's that damn rag?" he muttered.

He climbed down the loft ladder and went to stand at Nan's bedside. She lay under the clean sheets that Mrs Price had brought, dressed in her best lace-trimmed nightgown. She looked very clean and white.

He should feel sorrow, but all there was was panic. A great lump inside him seemed to block up his stomach. It stopped him thinking, stopped him crying. He was annoyed with her. How could she go and leave him like this? He wanted to shake her and make her come back.

"I need you, Nan . . . and now I think I've gone and lost William! What shall I do?"

He spoke out loud to her, and immediately felt a little better, for it was almost as though she'd answered him. He knew that the voice was only in his head, but it replied with all Nan's usual sharp common-sense. "Go and look for him, daft lad."

"Aye," he answered quickly and went downstairs.

Ben searched the cellars twice in case he'd missed a small frightened shape, crouching in the darkness. Then he went round the yard calling and peering into the worksheds. As he approached the grinding hull a nasty sense of apprehension came to him. Was that a faint scraping sound he heard? The grinders had long since gone to their homes. All at once he remembered the Book-Fuddler's note and felt in his pocket with trembling hands. The crumpled bit of paper was there and though it was too dark to see, Ben could remember well what it said.

He could not begin to work it all out but if William had

taken it into his head to hide in the grinding hull, he might be in very real trouble. Ben lifted the latch carefully, his heart thumping. He looked around the darkened workshop. Surely that was another scraping sound, and perhaps he saw the slipping away of a shadow, there at the back near the water trough. Ben gripped the sturdy wooden door frame so tightly that his fingers hurt. Whatever this shadowy nameless terror might be, he must make sure that William was not in there with it.

"William," he suddenly shouted. "William! Come to Ben. I'm not cross . . . not cross any more."

His voice sounded harsh and echoey. It was followed by silence; utter silence. Ben turned and pelted back to the safety of his own cottage.

He could hardly think straight at all. Frank was sitting with his head in his hands and Mrs Price was hovering by the fire.

"Found him?" his father asked, looking up.

Ben shook his head.

"Must be hiding somewhere. Scared, I daresay."

"Course he is," Mrs Price nodded, trying to comfort with bland agreement. "Turn up soon, for sure."

"No!" Ben shouted. Her very kindness made him furious. "No he won't. You don't know! I scared him, shouted at him. Told him he was bad."

"Now Ben!" His father frowned, pulled out of his own misery by such rudeness to a kindly neighbour.

"He was riding on her knee!" Ben pointed at Nan's chair, his hand shaking. "He was yelling for more . . . wouldn't stop. I was horrible to him! Blamed him! Scared him so he'll never, never come back!"

"Nay, Ben." His father was quickly on his feet, his arm about Ben's shoulders. "Let me think! What's best? Oh, how I wish Jess was here."

"Shall I run and fetch her?" said Ben, desperately wanting to do something . . . anything.

"We'll both go, if Mrs Price would be so kind?"

Jess and Ruth had gone to bed, but they were up and dressed in a moment. Jess was full of sorrow when she heard about Nan, but she took action as soon as she understood that William was missing. She boldly knocked up her neighbours and the darkest night was soon full of shouts and lanterns and rushlights. Some were sent into the woods, others headed off towards Sheffield and more walked down beside the river.

"Now," said Jess. "We've plenty of folk looking, let's try to think straight and clear about it. Where would the little lad run to? Who would he think of?"

"Mort!" Ben cried. How could he have been so stupid. "Mort and Dan. He'll have gone to the charcoal burners if he can find the way."

Without another word Ben snatched up Jess's lantern and ran off into the woods.

Ruth tried hard to follow him. "Wait," she called. "Wait for me!"

He turned and gratefully caught up her hand in his. They went on together, crashing through the undergrowth as fast as they could with only the flickering flame of the lantern and thin patches of moonlight to light their way. Once they blundered on to the wrong path, but quickly realised and set themselves right.

"We're there . . . almost there," Ben told her. He could hardly speak with the effort and urgency that he felt.

"Are you sure?" Ruth cried. "No fire . . . no lights?"

Ben ran out into the dark clearing, panting and desperate. "Where are they?" he yelled. "Damn them . . . damn them.

They've gone! Cleared off!"

They both wandered helplessly round the clearing, calling out William's name, as though their shouts might make him appear from the darkness. But they could see no sign of him, or the charcoal burners; not even the glowing embers of a fire.

At last Ben stood still and admitted the truth. "They've been gone for hours."

Ruth tripped over something soft as she walked across the charred earth. "What's this?" She stooped to pick it up and smelt it. "Oh Ben," she cried, reluctantly holding it up to the light of his lantern.

It was William's precious rag.

CHAPTER SEVENTEEN

The Sky Lit Up

Full well he knows what minds combin'd can do.
Full well maintains his birthright - he is free.

Ebenezer Elliott, The Sheffield Grinder

EN STARED down at the worn scrap of leather and all at once with a great gulping sound, he started to sob.

"He's gone," he cried. "My nan's gone and now William's gone."

"No . . . o," said Ruth. "No! It means that he was here. He's been here." She took hold of Ben firmly by the shoulders as though she'd shake him. "Don't! Don't cry now. You've got to think."

"Can't you see?" he told her through his tears. "They've taken him. He always wanted him . . . that Book-Fuddler! Lanky Dan!"

"Don't be so daft," Ruth came back at him with angry common sense. "He speaks his mind does Dan, but he'd never sneak a child away."

"He might!" said Ben, guilt flooding through him. "What if William came running here terrified, running away from me?"

"No, not even then. He'd carry the lad straight home to you. He'd say 'What are you doing to this bairn? Do you want him or not?'"

"Aye." Ben dashed the tears from his eyes. She was talking

132

sense. That was just what Dan would do.

"Think Ben!" Ruth insisted. "He's been here and found them gone. He'd be scared all right, but what would he do? Where would he go next?"

Ben tried to calm himself, ashamed of his weakness. Ruth was right; he must work it out. He must make himself imagine the small boy wandering frightened in the dark woods. He'd be cold and hungry. He'd be lost and lonely! Where would he think to go? Suddenly an idea came to him, though he shuddered a little at the thought.

"What is it? Tell me!" said Ruth.

"Old George," Ben said hesitantly.

"What? The charcoal burner's grave?"

"Aye." The more Ben thought about it, the more he was sure. "He's always dragging me through the woods to see poor George. It's not a fearful place to him. He'd play up there for hours if I'd let him. Come on, it's this way."

It was Ruth that hesitated now. "But it's so dark. I've never been there in the dark!"

Ben snatched up her hand again. "That's where he'll be," he spoke with certainty.

The dark shape of George Yardley's grave stood out clear and black in the misty moonlight. Ruth shrank back, trembling.

"There's nowt to fear," said Ben. "Listen! What's that?"

They stood still, scarce breathing, their hearts thumping fit to burst. In the distance they heard a faint shuffle. Then a dark smudgey shape moved beside George's grave.

"Poor George . . . poor Willum!" came a whimpering voice.

Suddenly tears were pouring down Ben's face again; he couldn't stop them. Strange harsh sounds threatened to burst from his throat; he wasn't sure whether they were sobs or laughter. He opened his mouth to shout out but stopped himself.

"Ruth," he whispered. "He might be scared of me. I was so horrid to him."

Ruth took hold of the lantern and though her hand shook, she strode bravely forward.

"William, William?" she called softly. "Here's Ruth come to find you."

He answered her; his voice faint and shivery. "Ben cross wi' me."

"No," said Ruth. "Ben's not cross with thee! Ben's sorry." She slipped the warm wool shawl from her shoulders and wrapped it round him. "Ben's here. He's come to take thee home."

"Home!" he repeated.

Ben followed Ruth's example, speaking gently as he moved forwards. "I'm right sorry," he said. "Please come home wi' me, William!"

He stooped to pick him up and caught sight of William's pale tear-smudged face in the yellow lantern light. He wanted to cry all over again when he felt the small ice-cold hands tighten around his neck and cling. It was the most comforting feeling in the world.

"Is it dinner?" said William.

"Yes," said Ben smiling through his tears. "It's dinner."

"Poor Nan?" said William.

"Yes, poor Nan," Ben replied.

Ben carried William back fast through the woods with Ruth trotting at their side. The feel of the warm lump on his back brought him great relief and energy.

"Are you sure we're on the right path?" Ruth asked.

"Aye," said Ben. "I can't get lost in these woods. The sound of the hammer is a grand help though. We could just do with hearing it now."

It was then that it happened. A rumble, loud as thunder, followed by a great bang and a flash. Flames went shooting up into the sky to the right of them.

Ben stopped, frozen still with the shock of it. Ruth gasped and caught at his arm. It was almost as if his wish for the sound of the hammers had been answered, but this was more terrifying than any hammer. They stared as the flames died down and a huge cloud of dust and smoke rose high above the treetops blotting out the moonlight.

William whimpered as they watched it.

"Oh save us!" Ruth cried. "What is it?"

Ben knew. He knew without the shadow of a doubt.

"It's the grinding hull," he said.

Ruth stared at him, unbelieving. The silence that followed the great bang was more dreadful than anything. Ben dumped William down and fished in his pockets again for the Book-Fuddler's letter.

"He warned me," he said. Holding the crumpled scrap of paper out towards Ruth. "He warned me and I never told my dad! Come on!" He snatched William up again. "We've got to get back."

"I'm scared," Ruth whispered. "Scared of what we'll find."

"Me too," Ben agreed. And though William was heavy on his back, he started to run towards the Scythe Works.

As soon as they stepped from the woods, they could see what had caused the noise and flames. A great gaunt hole stood where the gable end and the roof of the grinding hull should be. A cloud of dust hung over it all and a sharp smell of burning. Ben clapped a hand over his nose and mouth.

"Dad?" It came out more of a growl than a cry, his voice

thick and harsh with worry.

At least it looked as though the row of cottages still stood, though it was hard to see clearly. Ruth pulled up her apron and held it against her face. William began to cough. Ben swung him down to the ground and pulled off his own neckerchief. He tied it carefully around William's mouth and nose.

"Like this," he told him. "Like the grinders do."

"Like Dada!" said William obediently.

"It'll be all right," said Ben, wanting to soothe his own fears as much as William's. He took the child by the hand and led him into the smoke and dust.

The cottage appeared unharmed except for dust flying everywhere. They looked inside and called for Frank and Jess but got no reply. More than ever, Ben hated the thought of Nan lying so still up there in her bed while all this mess and chaos went on around her.

"There's folk in the yard," said Ruth. "I swear that I can hear the wheel turning."

They stepped warily round to the rubble of the grinding hull. The whole roof was off and slates had flown everywhere. It was hard to move without cracking them. Both the gable end walls were gone. Frank and Jess stood side by side, looking on bleakly as their master shuffled through the wheelswarf and debris in his night shirt and breeches. John Dyson stared grim-faced into the remains of his grinding hull. By the sounds of it, the water wheel was hurtling round wildly at great speed. Mrs Price and the Forgemaster tried to comfort the man, their voices low with concern.

Frank's face lit up for a moment when he saw that they'd got William safe. He swung William up into his arms and kissed him. "That's summat to be glad of this night," he said. "Oh, what a night!"

"What's that stink?" said Ben. The smell was overpowering and somehow familiar.

"Gunpowder," said Jess. "See here, there's burnt bits of wood and rag. We think a whole barrel of the stuff's gone up. Thank God there's nobody hurt!"

"But who . . .?" Ben started, then he suddenly knew. His question was cut off short by a sharp look from his father.

The Forgemaster spoke gently. "Come now Mr Dyson, sir. We'd best get that wheel stopped."

John Dyson stared at him for a moment as though he'd not heard, then he seemed to shake himself a little and nod. "Yes. I daresay you're right."

Frank stayed to help the men set about fixing the wheel and Jess took William from him. "Back to the cottage," she said. "We must see to this little un."

Jess warmed up broth and made them all drink a little. William did not object when Ben led him up to bed; though he insisted on going to stand quietly beside Nan for a moment. William was too used to death to be afraid. He touched her cold cheek.

"Gone . . . Dada," he said.

"Yes," Ben whispered gently. "She's gone. Just like your Daddy."

Ben and Ruth sat up round the fire with Jess and Frank; it seemed that none of them could sleep and dawn light was showing through the window.

"Was this what Mary Ann warned of?" Ben asked at last.

"I think so," said Jess. "I told them I'd have nothing to do with any harm that they planned. I'd do nothing more and I'd know nothing more, but it's clear this is no accident! Mary Ann warned of trouble and now it's come. It's almost a relief,

I swear it is. Though there's a terrible mess and hardship, at least nobody's hurt. I made them promise that!"

"He tried to warn me," said Ben, pulling out the Book-Fuddler's note. "I never thought he'd do anything as bad as this."

Jess took the note and read it.

"It wasn't him," she said. "It wasn't Lanky Dan that blew up our hull. You mustn't think that."

Ben sighed with relief. "I did think it might be him. He seemed to know everything."

"No," said Jess. "He was our messenger. He came and went through the woods in his secret way, and carried news back and forth. No, I don't know exactly who it is that's done this and I don't want to know."

"I carried a message once," said Ben.

"There's a lot of us been carrying messages," said Jess. "Do you know? I almost felt sorry for John Dyson, standing there in all the muck and wheelswarf, looking so puzzled and saying nowt. Why would he not listen?"

"What will he do now?" Ruth asked.

"I suppose he'll get his grinding hull built up again," Frank told her. "I daresay he'll have his insurance money to pay for it. But still – he'll not have grinders working there for quite a while."

"He'll have to get the Thorpe Brothers to let him use their wheel again," said Ben. "He'll not like that."

"Aye. It's back to them when he's stuck," said Frank. "I know it's hard but I think we should try to get a bit of rest. We've much to do tomorrow. I'd be glad if you and Ruth would stay with us, Jess. I can make myself comfortable on the settle if you two would use my bedroom."

"We'll be glad to stay, if you wish it," said Jess.

CHAPTER EIGHTEEN

Whatever Troubles May Come . . .

High, high above the tree-tops
The lark is soaring free;
Where streams the light through broken clouds
His speckled breast I see:

Beneath the might of wicked men
The poor man's worth is dying;
But, thank'd be God, in spite of them
The lark still warbles flying!

Ebenezer Elliott

OVER THE NEXT few days the Scythe Works was one great mess of muddle and confusion. Some of the forgemen attempted to carry on their work as their master asked, while others turned to the task of clearing up. There were two constables and an insurance inspector wandering through the dust and rubble, asking questions, writing down notes and generally getting in everyone's way.

None of it touched Ben or his father, for now that the terror of the explosion was over, they turned their thoughts back to Nan.

The loss of the tough old woman who'd cared for them was greater than any damaged wall or roof or grinding hull could ever be. In the days that followed they missed her bitterly. Even

William was quiet and lost, but sometimes he'd curl himself up in Nan's rocking chair and sing in a small sad voice:

"Bye baby . . . rock,
Bye baby rock.
Up in the treetops,
All fall down."

He'd sing away as he rocked back and forth, getting all the words jumbled. Ben's eyes filled up with tears at the sight and sound of him.

Jess spent much of her time in the Sterndales' cottage, helping in every way she could. Whenever they were hungry, there she was, baking bread. Whenever they were puzzled, she told them what to do. She set about organising Nan's funeral and fixed up their Sunday best clothes. She baked and cooked and carried round the ale at the funeral feast.

The Scythe Works was stilled, and all the workers came dressed in their best to follow Nan's funeral procession. Most of them had known the sharp-tongued old lady for years and remembered her with fondness. Even John Dyson came in his tall black hat and walked in the procession looking distracted and sorrowful. It was only after he'd sipped his ale at the feast and returned to his house that the rumours began.

"Turned him down! Turned him down flat," said Elsie.

"What's that?"

"Who turned him down?"

"The insurance company," Elsie was red-cheeked and flustered with her news.

"Nay," said Frank.

"That's what I've heard. Oh, he seemed to think he was insured, but they say it was never fixed up properly!"

Whispers and doubts ran all through the gathering. There

was much concern and worry for if John Dyson's business failed, what would happen to his workers?

"Why would the man not listen to Mary Ann?"

"Heaven help us all!"

"Ooh . . . I thought he looked pale!"

"Whatever's coming next?"

Mrs Price spoke low to Jess as she passed her the spiced mourning cakes on a polished wooden trencher. "Have you heard about the arrest?"

"Nay," cried Jess. "What's this now?"

"Aye," Forgemaster Price nodded solemnly. "They've arrested the two Thorpe brothers and another chap who's a friend of theirs. Strong union men all three of them!"

"What? For the explosion?"

"That's it! There's some talk of a barrel of gunpowder seen up at the Cutler's Arms in Sheffield. You know those brothers are always there, chatting to Mrs Green."

"Is it true do you think?"

The Forgemaster shrugged his shoulders. "Who can tell! I doubt we'll be using their grinding wheel again."

Late that night Ruth and Jess sat round the fire along with Ben and his father. They had talked themselves to a standstill, voicing their fears for the future. William fell asleep on Jess's knee and none of them had the heart to disturb him.

"We should be on our way," said Jess wearily, but she made no move to get up.

"Aye," said Ruth, sighing and sitting there staring into the fire.

"Well," said Frank, shifting in his chair and flushing a little. "Maybe tha'd stay?"

"I suppose so," said Jess yawning and blinking. "But I'm

thinking that settle's awful hard for thee to be sleeping on."

"It is," said Frank. He sat forward now, rubbing his hands together nervously. He coughed and spoke quickly. "It's terrible hard is that settle, but . . . what I'm thinking is . . . maybe tha'd stay for good."

Jess looked up at him sharply now and William stirred on her lap. At last she saw how tense and fearful the man was.

"I'm hoping it's not disrespectful to my mother to speak of such a thing on her funeral day, but . . . I'm thinking that maybe thee and me could be wed? Though what with Dyson's troubles and losses, I've little to offer thee. I've maybe no work or wages. I daresay it looks as though I'm just needing thee to see to the bairns!" He whispered it all in a rush, his voice faint and hoarse with worry.

Ben caught his breath and stared open-mouthed across at Ruth.

"That's quite a speech, Frank," said Jess. "I don't think I've ever heard thee make such a speech before!"

Then suddenly she was exploding with happy laughter. William was wide awake and struggling to the floor, unsure that he liked this treatment.

"Ey, tha's a daft one, Frank Sterndale," Jess cried. "I've been waiting for thee to ask me these last two years. I'd thought I'd have to do the asking myself before long! Of course I'll wed thee. We can't have thee sleeping on a hard wooden plank for ever!"

"Oh lor!" Frank was weak and shaking with relief.

Jess got up and put her arms around him. "Whatever troubles may come to us, we'll face them together, my dear."

"Hurray!" cried Ruth.

At once the small room was filled with laughing and crying. William was wild-eyed at the sight of them leaping about and hugging each other. Ben snatched him up from Nan's rag rug where he crouched.

"Tha's going to have a mother!" he cried. "I'm going to have a mother!"

"He's going to be my own little brother!" yelled Ruth. She covered William's head with kisses until he squirmed and shouted for her to stop. But Ruth was not finished yet, she turned to Ben. "Tha'll be my brother too."

"Will tha like it?" he asked her, his cheeks burning.

"Oh yes," she said. "I'll like it fine," and she kissed him so that he blushed even more.

"Eh dear," said Jess wiping the corner of her eye. "What a to do! I hope it's not wrong to be so happy on a day of mourning! I don't know what your nan would have said."

"I do. I always know just what she'd have said," Ben told them. "She'd have thought it a grand thing for us all, then she'd have told us to calm ourselves down and get off to our beds."

"Well?" said Jess, smiling at him. "That sounds like good sense to me, and if I'm to be your mother now, tha must do as I tell thee."

"And what's that?" asked Ben.

"Off to our beds at once and not another word tonight."

"Come on, William," said Ben snatching up his hand. "We must do as our mother says."

Author's Note

DYSON'S SCYTHE WORKS are now known as the Abbeydale Hamlet, an industrial museum on the south side of Sheffield. John Dyson, the owner in the year 1842 was resented by the Grinders' Union for using non-Union workers. Early in the morning of November 7th 1842 an explosion took place which blew off the gable ends and roof of the grinding hull. George and John Thorpe and William Hopkinson were accused. A trial took place, but nothing could be proved and the three men were acquitted.

Mr Price was the real forgemaster at Dyson's Works, according to the 'Sheffield and Rotherham Independent' Nov 19th 1842.

Ben, his family and the other workers in Dyson's Yard are fictional characters, though there would have been a cellar lad, a potman, a melter and a puller-out all employed in the Works.

The Book-Fuddler is not entirely my own invention. In Dorothy Thompson's book, 'The Chartists', she quotes a Nottinghamshire shoemaker:

'He was what is known to the literary craftsmen as a "book-fuddler" that is to say, when exhausted by close application to his work, instead of resorting to the shop's meeting-house to drink and brawl and smoke . . . he would wander through the streets and lanes . . . of the City and West End, where old books were found in super-abundance, and where he could revel in the luxury of the best writers . . . I have known many shopmates of this stamp.'

Samuel Holberry was a young Sheffield Chartist who was imprisoned after a planned rebellion was discovered. The parts of the story that relate to his funeral and to the summer of 1842 are as accurate as I could make them.

The lines of poetry that I have used to head some of the chapters are by Ebenezer Elliott 1781-1849, a Sheffield poet best known for his People's Anthem which now appears in many hymn books. He was also known as the Corn Law Rhymer, for his determined opposition to the Corn Laws or Bread Tax.

There is no record of John Dyson having received 'Mary Ann' warning messages in 1842, though this was the custom in South Yorkshire at the time. Mary Ann letters are recorded as having been sent to the Tyzack family at Abbeydale Scythe Works in 1858 – John Dyson's successors.

Where does this tradition come from? During the French Revolution a new symbol was needed to replace the King. A female character from French tradition was brought forward. She represented the Spirit of Freedom. She appears in much of the revolutionary artwork as a beautiful young woman, wearing a peasant's red liberty cap, and carrying the spear of revolution. She was called Marianne. Revolutionaries dressed in women's clothes and called themselves Marianne to disguise their true identity. Revolutionary placards and posters appeared signed Marianne. Although I cannot find written proof of it, I am convinced that Mary Ann was our 'down to earth' South Yorkshire version of the French spirit of Freedom – Marianne.

Acknowledgements

THE AUTHOR particularly wishes to thank Janet Peatman, Keeper of the Abbeydale Industrial Hamlet, for her kind help and encouragement throughout this project.

Also thanks to Peter Bennett – Former Keeper of the Hamlet – and Bernard Callan for sharing their knowledge of the history of steel making.

Linda Jepson and Sue Sinclair for sharing their research on the Hamlet.

Bill and Gladys Brookes for advice and encouragement.

The author and publishers would like to thank the following: the Abbeydale Industrial Hamlet for permission to reproduce the bill-head of Dyson's Works in Abbeydale (frontispiece); Sheffield City Museum for 'South East View of Sheffield' 1854 by William Ibbitt (p. 57); Sheffield Local Studies Library for 'Making Crucibles for Melting' & 'Treading the Clay' (p. 24), 'Casting Ingots' and 'Drawing Crucibles' (p. 37), and 'Casting Crucible Steel' (p. 106), all from *The Illustrated Exhibitor*, August 23, 1851, and 'Scythe-Grinding' (p. 78) from *The Illustrated London News*; also for the photograph on p. 16 of the Charcoal Burner's Grave, (Sheffield Photographic Society).